# AUTHOR'S COMMENTS

The characters in this novel are entirely fictional. The locations are intended to be accurate unless modified to fit the story. The descriptions of technological, agricultural, and scientific events are generally accurate except where it suits the author's story to modify reality.

I wish to thank my wife, Joann, for not minding the hours I have spent in front of the word processor with this story. I also want to thank Joann for being my first reader and my first copyeditor. In addition I want to recognize the suggestions provided by the Manatee Community College Writers Workshop. They were kind enough to listen to the reading of three selected chapters.

Actually, I have found the writing of this story an enjoyable activity. Since my retirement from the academic world I have appreciated the opportunity to write something different than textbooks, articles, and lecture notes.

When I began this story I did not have a solution to the murder. I began with a murder in the Opera House. The story evolved from there. For almost a year the work sat idle because I did not have a reasonable way figured out to end the story with some sense of rationality. Finally with just a bit of tweaking reality, the resolution became apparent.

D1523417

# SYDNEY, AUSTRALIA

The double ring of the telephone startled Jeff Spencer from the concentration of unpacking his two suitcases. Stumbling over his unpacked carry-on bag, he reached past his portable lap top computer sitting next to the repeatedly ringing telephone.

"Hello," Jeff said, with surprise. How could anyone be calling him yet. He had just arrived from Sydney airport after the ungodly 13 1/2 hour flight from Los Angeles.

"G'Day," a familiar female voice replied over the telephone. "Welcome to Sydney and down under," the voice continued.

"Aaron, how did you know I was in?" Jeff asked.

"An editor's hunch," Aaron Worthington replied. " You know, you did send me an E-mail note telling me you were arriving today. I used the internet to check with the airlines and found Qantas flight 11 arriving this morning at 6:45 a.m. Allowing for casual stumbling off the plane, harried luggage pick up, delay after delay at immigration and customs, the forty minute ride on the Air Shuttle, and hotel check-in I concluded you would be walking into your room at this moment."

"Good investigative journalism," Jeff replied. "You were close. Customs was a breeze. I took a cab rather than the shuttle. So, I'm almost unpacked. But, you can imagine what has happened to my body clock. What time is it really?" he asked, sliding into a chair exhausted.

"Good heavens, it's 9:30 a.m. Let's do lunch. I'll pick up some take away and meet you in the rose garden at the Botanic Garden at 12:15. Don't fall asleep," Aaron said with that editor's commanding tone which she knew irked Jeff.

"I'll do what I can to stay awake. You know I can't sleep on an airplane. Did you locate tickets for the concert at the Opera House?

"No worries," replied Aaron. "Tickets for tonight. It's the last performance."

"I'll never be able to stay awake."

1

"I'll poke you in the ribs. See you for lunch at 12:15."

Jeff always liked to go to the Opera House on every research trip he made to Australia. He relied on Aaron to obtain good tickets for whatever was playing. Good seats were always gone by the time he arrived. Aaron never failed to use her journalistic contacts to have good seats for a concert or opera. She preferred the opera. Jeff preferred the concert. He could sit through anything in the Opera House just to experience the shear beauty and marvelous acoustics. This was one way Aaron endeared herself to Jeff. Jeff returned the favor when Aaron could make it to the United States. He always knew she wanted to take a trip through the beautiful Napa Valley. Nice quid pro quo, he thought.

Now, to stay awake. Make his body adjust to the sixteen hour time change. His usual routine was to take a walk, visit a gallery or museum, lunch, stroll downtown or jog along Circle Quay, read the local papers at the library, place two dollars on the weirdest name horse racing, nice dinner, and crash.

The next day he would begin serious work. That meant a trip to one or more of the universities to discuss some of the latest scientific research. He would work two days and be a tourist every third day. With that schedule he could obtain the latest bio-genetic research or mechanical application work to satisfy his readers back in the United States.

Jeff had become a successful free lance writer. All sorts of news media sought his stories. Some stories he syndicated. Other stories he sold as exclusives. After graduating from Medill School of Journalism at Northwestern University Jeff had worked as a writer for two newspapers and a couple of environmentally oriented scientific organizations. He liked the freedom of being a 'free-lancer.'

Over the last three years he had developed specialization in state of the art technical innovations. He had been in Melbourne Australia when Latrobe University had pioneered the medical research which led to in-vitro fertilization. He was in Scotland shortly after a sheep was successfully cloned.

Today was Monday. It was recovery day. Jeff had just over two hours before meeting Aaron in the Botanic Garden. Time to walk through Hyde Park to the state art gallery and check out the latest special display and then the short walk across the street from the gallery to the Botanic Garden. The roses should be gorgeous. He hoped Aaron would have some Aussie meat pies rather than McDonalds burgers or Pizza Hut. He liked Aussie fast food. Aussies were on a craze for American fast food burgers and pizzas. What a shame.

As Jeff walked through the lobby of the art gallery, he noticed the mixture of nationalities of people in the gallery. Australia had become every bit as much an ethnic melting pot as the United States.

"Can I help you?" asked the strolling security person. She seemed pleasant but firm.

"No, thanks. I'm on my way to the main exhibition hall. I want to see what is featured."

"Oh, you'll like the Herman Gerhard landscape work display," the security guard replied. "He catches the spirit of the rural outback. Even captures the spirit of the Aboriginal dreamtime in his latest work."

Jeff strolled on into the main exhibit room. Gerhard's work was interesting. Jeff had seen some of his work on site during his last trip up into the Darling Downs wheat country. So he was now working with Aboriginals in the landscape. That certainly would be extending the scope of his work. Jeff began systematically working his way from left to right around the room just the way Gerhard's work was chronologically displayed.

Gerhard was unique in the way he included the aboriginal people in his landscapes. Earlier artists had 'placed' the native peoples in scenes as artifacts. Earliest versions provided a pejorative view of the aboriginal. Gerhard's aboriginals were an integral part of his landscapes. They looked like they belonged.

3

*George E. Tuttle*

Jeff reminded himself he must pace himself. Don't dawdle too long at any section. Must make it to the Botanic Rose Garden by 12:15.

# NORTH SYDNEY

On the ferry crossing from North Sydney to downtown Sydney, a courier clutched an insulated case containing four small bottles of liquid. Stanley Hutch had no idea what was in the bottles. In his pocket he carried a small brown envelope. The envelope contained a 3 1/2 inch computer disk. Stanley suspected it was a computer disk but he had not been told.

Stanley currently worked for TRANSCOM Courier and Delivery Service (TCDS). He was recently retired. No! Forced out! 'Buy out' they called it. 'Corporate re-organization' they said. He had worked for Johnson Printing Supplies for 25 years after returning from the war. With his veteran's pension and his buy out he could manage for some time. But, he wasn't eligible yet for superannuation. Thus, he was forced to take a job. Nobody wanted a 50 year old ex soldier who worked in the printing supply business. Too old to retrain. Too young to quit. His job with TRANSCOM was the best he could do. It paid him enough to live meagerly.

He saved to do two things. One day each month he went to the race track and spent $20 betting the horses. Only $20. He was disciplined. When he lost his money he just watched the horses and the people. Usually the horses were more interesting. His other great pleasure was two or three days each month he went to a concert at the Opera House. Stanley loved the music.

Today, Stanley's job was to carry this small package from the laboratory at Macquarie University to the National Research Laboratory in Canberra. His pick up was at 4:00 p.m. Too late to make it to the train station to make the last bus to Canberra. He would go to Canberra first thing in the morning. He had picked up the brown envelope at Bengotti Imports at their headquarters in St. Leonards. So he had decided to take the ferry to Circle Quay and then the bus to his small home at Bondi Beach.

Stanley didn't bother to search for a seat on the busy ferry. The ride was a short one and he wanted to remain near the exit.

"Oh, excuse me," a young lady said bumping into Stanley as she moved past. She reached awkwardly and placed her hand on the insulated case. He did not feel the very subtle hand slide into his jacket pocket. Just as she began to remove the envelope the ferry swerved in its approach to the dock at Circle Quay. Afraid of discovery she withdrew her hand from his jacket pocket.

"That's all right miss. Please don't bump my package. It might break."

"Sorry."

Stanley knew it was no harm meant, but he was told to be very careful with the package. The clerk at the Macquarie University lab made a big point of how fragile it might be and how important it was.

The ferry was about to dock.

"Passengers please wait until the boat is docked before moving to an exit," barked the loud speaker.

Might as well be talking to the trees he thought. Everyone was already moving toward the side where the exit ramp would be dropped. Stanley grabbed the package and held it protectively against his side pocket containing the brown envelope, He kept the package protected as he was slowly propelled along by the moving mass of people.

A thud and the side of the ferry nudged against the pier. The exit ramp was dropped a second before the throng of rushing humanity carried Stanley off the ferry, along the walk way through the terminal. At last he stumbled out onto the moving throng of rush hour workers and tourists streaming past the terminal.

Stanley had to navigate his way across twelve lanes of moving people to reach the street and cross over to catch his bus which would take him to his home in the suburb of Bondi Beach.

"Excuse me, sir." he said as he moved between two people moving in different directions. He had learned the survival move from years of commuting to and from work. It was routine.

"Excuse me."

"Watch it."

"Sorry, mam"

"Pleeease."

"Excuse me, lady." Stanley could still keep a civil tongue. Some of the people moving through the throng did and some didn't.

Finally, he made it through and came to rest against the wall of the corner tourist shop. He would rest a moment and catch his breath before joining another throng crossing to the busses waiting along Pitt Street to take up much of the moving swarm and disperse them to dozens of points around Sydney and its near suburbs. Others would head into the train station to take the loop train to other stations like Wynyard, Town Hall, or Central to disperse to various suburbs. The whole Circle Quay area had become a transportation re-distribution center. Some thought it had become aesthetically distracting from the natural beauty of the harbor.

As he paused and rested against the building he watched the sights around him. In front an aborigine played a didjeridu. The haunting sound was unsettlingly eerie. Before it took his mind into some strange dreamstate his attention was diverted to a woman trying to give away bibles. Across from her was a sleazy looking man watching each person she approached. As she got someone's attention long enough for them to look at the bible, the sleazy man swept past making a quick move into one of their pockets. This time he came away empty handed. But, Stanley knew there would be a next time.

Stanley Hutch needed to move. His bus was about to depart. There would be another in 15 minutes. But, he needed to catch this one because he was going home to leave his deliveries for first thing tomorrow, change, and return as quickly as possible. He had a ticket for tonight's symphony concert at the Opera House.

To Stanley the ticket had cost dearly, and he didn't want to miss the concert. They were playing Beethoven tonight. He loved Beethoven. The power of the music gave him a good feeling.

7

He made the dash across the street and squeezed onto his bus, number 224. As usual, standing room only. He was the tenth standee. More than 10 and the driver shut the door. Metro ordinance. The drivers union enforced it literally.

Thirty minutes later, Stanley departed in Bondi Beach and walked the three blocks to his small home. Most homes in the Bondi community were small. They had been quaint family homes built for World War II veterans who wanted to live near the beach. Some had deteriorated as the beach became more of a recreation center for greater Sydney. Stanley had purchased his small neat home when it came on the market. He had kept it up nicely. Repaired. And, painted. Other houses nearby were also being refurbished. Bondi was rebounding as a neighborhood.

Upon entering, he noticed he had four messages on his phone answering machine. He would listen later. Carefully, he placed the package with the four small bottles securely in a box in his closet. He had to hurry to dress and return by bus to downtown Sydney for the 8:00 Symphony concert at the Opera House.

Stanley changed pants, shirt, and shoes. He would wear the same jacket. He forgot the brown envelope with the computer disk was still in his pocket.

No time to eat. He would grab a Big Mack at the corner before catching his bus. He did not want to miss tonight's concert. Stanley loved the Sydney Symphony. Even more, he loved to hear them play in the Concert Hall at the Sydney Opera House. Tonight they were playing all classical music. The program scheduled was not only the Beethoven he loved but also Tschaikovsky. And, the 1812 Overture no less. He really did not want to miss this evening.

# KANSAS CITY

At 6:00 p.m. Monday evening in Sydney Australia it was 3:00 a.m. Monday morning in Kansas City. Martin White was struggling with his house key. The blond with him, Cindy Nelson, was an assistant states attorney in Kansas City, Kansas, who found it more convenient to live in Kansas City, Missouri. They had started with dinner, a club show, dancing at a jazz bar, helped close down a country line dance club. If either one had driven after the club show they might have been DUI. Not good for the reputation of a well known feature writer with the Kansas City Star or a young assistant states attorney, even if it were in another state. They left his car and took a taxi. Tonight it would be his condo.

"Damn, the key won't work," White growled.

"Honey, you might have the wrong key," Cindy whispered breathing in his ear.

"Just a minute."

"Take your time, we have all night."

""The night's half over. There I found the key." Martin opened the door and they both stumbled in.

"Some coffee?" White asked.

"No way," Cindy purred. She was already out of her blouse and shoes.

"Listen Cindy, I have to get some sleep. I have to go in and work on that story tomorrow. I need to wrap up this wheat blight story. It's dynamite."

"Let's make our own explosion, then we'll see about sleep." Her skirt was on the floor and she was pulling Martin by the arm into the bedroom. There was an explosion in Martin White's condo that night.

Martin and Cindy's relationship had evolved. They met at a Kansas City marathon race. Both were 'athletic thirty somethings.' After finishing a grueling 10K run they struck up a conversation. Then they discovered they had more in common

9

than running. They liked the same movies and the same foods. The relationship had gone just so far and stalemated. Neither wanted marriage. At least not yet.

Martin's career had taken him from small town reporting of city meetings and school boards to an opportunity to investigate fraud in a regional agricultural stabilization office. From that award winning piece he had made the move to the Kansas City Star. He now had a bigger beat. He had become the expert of reporting on national interest agriculture stories. It might be breakthroughs in seed genetics to satellite assisted wheat planting.

Cindy's career after law school had also taken off. She began in Kansas City and several high profile cases she won as a public defender had gotten her the opportunity to switch from public defender to assistant prosecutor. Changing tables in the courtroom was a hard decision for her to make. She still cared about the rights of individuals. But, now she was prosecuting abusive parents and spouses. She felt she was still defending the "little people." But, she now did it on behalf of the people.

Cindy and Martin's careers kept them so busy they had not been able to make the leap to marriage. They were in fact a 'happy couple' in spite of not yet making the trip down the aisle.

Martin woke to the smell of fresh coffee. He crawled out of bed holding his splitting head.

"Coffee, honey? It will help that headache." Cindy was dressed, and had a fresh pot of coffee ready. She knew where he stored his beans in the refrigerator to keep them fresh. She knew just how strong he liked coffee for a hang over. She liked it the same way.

"I don't think the caffeine really helps. It's all mental."

"Right. Here's to a cup of mental pleasure." She handed Martin his coffee.

He took a sip, then a long sip, finally half the cup. He reached in the cupboard for a box of fresh strawberry coffee cake. "Here, have some calorie free coffee cake."

"Calorie free my eye; but, I'll have some calories with my caffeine. So, what's the big wheat story you are doing."

Martin wasn't awake enough yet to really welcome a long discussion about work. But, he knew what she was doing. She was forcing him to actively engage his brain and that would help him wake up and shake the hangover. It also helped her.

"Well, I covered a speaker at the ag extension meeting the other day. Seems there is some devilish rust invading the wheat fields in eastern Colorado and western Kansas. They said it may threaten this year's crop. Farmers faced big potential economic losses. Farmers would be hurt. Foreign contracts would not be filled. Prices of food would likely go sky high. The situation could be a disaster for Kansas and not good for the United States.This could be a very big story."

"Don't they have some chemical which will attack the rust?" She asked.

"No one knows what to do. The ag and bio big brains at KU in Lawrence are stymied. They don't have a clue where the rust is coming from or how it works. They fear something might have mutated. You know, some DNA gene curled the wrong way or some damn thing."

"What will happen?" asked Cindy.

"Oh, the agriculture researchers will find some solution. They will take some test samples from plants, identify cell structures, and then run some hypothetical computer models."

"You mean solve it with a computer?"

"Yes and no. Yes, they will have a few hypothetical solutions. But, no they will not know for sure which solution will work."

"How do they find out which solution will work?"

"Basically by trial and error. That means growing some lab samples and finding what combinations of cell behavior is modified by particular chemicals or combinations of chemicals."

"How long will that take?"

"It could take days or weeks."

"And, if weeks a lot of the crop could be lost in the fields?"

"That's right," replied Martin.

"Isn't there any short cut?"

"Not unless they get a lucky breakthrough. If they get a break they could drastically shortcut the process. They could significantly speed up the computer modeling without having to grow a lot of trail and errors."

"So, days instead of weeks?" asked Cindy.

"Right. Days instead of weeks. It might be enough to save most of the crops already infected as well as prevent the infection of others. Once the spread is stopped, the crisis would be over."

"Research can do wonders."

"Only if there is a breakthrough."

Martin reached for another piece of coffee cake and a refill of coffee. "Don't you have cases pending today?"

"Court isn't in session until noon today. One of the superior judges is having a birthday today. Justice will have to wait till noon. I do need to make an appearance sometime. You know, smile and press the flesh. Why don't you take a cab to the Star, I'll take a cab to pick up your car where we left it, I'll drive the car to the Star and park it in your spot, then I'll take a taxi to my place, freshen up, and make my appearance at the judge's birthday party before noon."

Martin looked at Cindy for a long time. Then he said, "sounds just like a lawyer. You have the plan all put together. Great by me."

# ST. LEONARDS

Frank Bengotti sat at his desk in the third floor of Bengotti Imports in St. Leonards, a north suburb of Sydney. He sat at a computer terminal looking intently at inventory records. He frowned as he realized they were running low on exotic nursery plants. Their suppliers deep in the interior of Indonesia dealt only with Frank and Al (Alphonse) Bengotti because Bengotti Imports had a "lock" on shipping routes through the jungle to the docks. Younger brother Renaldo oversaw the Indonesian supply and research part of the business. Renaldo was the research expert.

Bengottis had cornered the market on some of the most exotic plants. Bengotti Imports shipped all over Australia through an elaborate network. Plants were fragile and had to be shipped quickly. Bengottis had pioneered a computerized communication network with themselves as communication manager between retail outlets and the jungle sources. Laptop computers could go anywhere. Same day distribution occurred once plants were picked up in jungle shipping locations. The actual source of plants was a guarded secret.

But, Frank knew their major competitor, Wuan Imports, was getting close to finding their locations. They kept the locations, names, phone numbers well coded in their data banks. They changed the codes monthly. The code breaking data were transported monthly on a simple floppy disk to their several outlets in Canberra, Melbourne, Brisbane, and Wollongong.

Wuan Imports did not have the distribution and communication advantage of Bengottis. Wuan Imports took ten days from order to arrival of the product at retail outlets. No matter how good the shipping conditions, the plants were of lesser quality than Bengottis Imported plants.

Frank's brother, Alphonse entered. "Frank, you look worried."

"Yea, we need to make another shipment. Our inventories at all of our outlets are low," Frank replied.

"Frank, our outlets can place their own orders direct. All we do is relay those orders through cyberspace in a matter of seconds. Don't worry."

"Yeah, but we usually assume everyone will order in mid cycle between our code change dates. We just changed codes and sent a new disk by courier to each city. It will be another four days until everything is in place to reorder."

"Frank, we aren't that close on inventory are we," Al asked with a concerned look.

"Yes, we are," relied Frank. Our outlets in Melbourne and Brisbane may be all right; but, Canberra, Wollongong, and Sydney are very short. It will take four days for shipments to arrive after we place orders to our suppliers in the jungles." It required three days through the jungle and one day by air transport to destination.

"We messed up, Frank," growled Al. "How did that happen?"

"We were both gone, remember. You didn't check before you left. I didn't check. It shouldn't happen; but, it did."

Frank, Alphonse, and Renaldo Bengotti had built the business almost from scratch. Both had grown up in immigrant homes in Sydney. Their parents had left Italy in the turmoil of politics in the 1950s. Then the boys were two, four, and six years of age.

Frank, Al, and Renaldo grew up in Italian homes in an adopted land. Like generations of immigrants to Australia Frank and Al Bengotti became amalgamated into their adopted land. Their parents encouraged them to learn English, at least the Australian version of English.

Frank and Al went to college for two years and then into the Australian military to serve in Vietnam. In Nam they learned a lot about the jungle, technology, communication, and getting along. Renaldo missed Nam but he had finished college in the United States majoring in bio-chemistry at UCLA.

14

The Bengotti boys returned home in 1972, bought a defunct nursery, a couple of trucks, two retail outlets in Sydney and began creating their empire. Within ten years they had created the nursery empire they still operated today. They had worked hard and mostly within the law for what they had. They were not willing to roll over for any challenge which came along.

Bengottis had the corner on the market for several years. As often happens in an open market system, one company's success attracts competitors. Wuan Imports had begun a local business seven years ago. Three years ago Wuans had entered the international market. They had gotten a large capitol infusion from somewhere. No one really knew where.

There had been some evidence that Wuans agents had been shadowing Bengotti operations in Indonesia and they definitely had been watching retail operations in several cities in Australia. Bengottis knew they had competition. Bengottis assumed that the Wuans were trying to move into their market. But, Bengottis had been able to stay ahead because of their ability to deliver better plants faster to customers.

# SYDNEY

Jeff Spencer opened his hotel room door  recognizing Aaron's four rap knock. She entered the room and threw her arms around Jeff.

"Jeff, it's been months since I saw you," Aaron finally said after a long kiss.

"Yea, you were attending that editors conference in San Francisco. Missed, you," Jeff replied.

"Tell me about your trip over."

"It was boring. What can you say about 13 3/4 hours in an airplane from Los Angles. Both movies were oldies. At least the food wasn't too bad. It was hard to remember not to drink caffeine or alcohol. But you know the routine. You've made the same flight."

"Let me freshen up before we go to dinner. It has been a hectic day since I had lunch with you in the rose garden."

"Normally I would just crash tonight after the long flight."

"Jeff, I know. But this is the last night of the symphony performances and I knew you would want to go."

"Of course Aaron. If I can just stay awake after dinner. I don't want to miss Beethoven or Tschaikovsky."

Jeff sank into the sofa and watched ABC news while Aaron went about taking a quick shower. They left and began the leisurely walk to the Opera House.

They soon found themselves part of the crowd walking along the Circle Quay toward the Opera House. Most were tourists at this time. They were on their way to dinner at the Bennelong Restaurant at the Opera House. Most of those attending the symphony  would arrive later.

They were seated at a harbor side table in the restaurant where they could watch the dozens of boats on the harbor as they began their leisurely meal with a bottle of Rosemont Estate Suriz wine. Aaron had introduced Jeff to some of the best of Australia's greatest wines. Rosemont Estate Shiraz was one of the best. It's dry tingly flavor lit up the taste buds better than any other medium red wine. Jeff returned the favor for Aaron when she came to California. He introduced her to some Napa Valley's best. Their sharing each others favorite quality wine demonstrated the depth of their relationship which transcended 11,000 miles.

"So, tell me about the hectic day at the Herald," Jeff said smiling at Aaron.

"Oh, the usual. What kind of focus can we give to the information we have about the events in our world. The economy is getting better; so, we can either be up beat and tell how good it is; or, we can run those stories from all the Cassandras telling us this is just the short upturn before the economy totally collapses with a big ugly depression."

"Well, which is it?" Jeff asked with a smile.

"Who knows. You know the business. Any kind of facts we want are out there. What kind of story do we want to tell?"

"So, what story do you want to tell to Australia and the rest of the world which reads the Herald?"

"We think feeling up beat is the national mood. That's what will sell newspapers, which sells advertising, which is how we make money. The same way those papers in Chicago, San Francisco, and wherever else you sell your stories to make their money."

They continued their meal with a steady line of the same professional banter. They were both good at what they did. Jeff thought about Aaron's success and the editorial awards she had garnered in five years with the Herald. She was a recognized professional in Australia. Jeff knew he was equally successful as a free lance writer in the United States. Several of his stories had also been syndicated around the world. But, his base was in the United States. His professional success and Aaron's professional success meant they had not been able to have a closer relationship. Their relationship was warm and close but six to seven months out of the year they never saw each other. She was in Sydney and he was in San Francisco. Their faithful computers communicated on their behalf weekly or even oftener. Neither one knew for sure what was going to be the future of their relationship.

The many hues of light in Sydney Harbor anchored the green glowing lights which lit up the Sydney Harbor bridge. The big "coat hanger," the Aussies called it. Jeff and Aaron continued their discussion of their respective lives as they were served rack of lamb and barramundi. They finished their meal with another Hunter Valley red wine favorite, Lindemans Cabernet Sauvignon by tipping their wine glasses and watching the green "coat hanger" across the water.

Leaving the Bennelong Restaurant at the Opera House, Jeff and Aaron made their way upstairs into the Concert Hall venue and then into their seats in the concert hall. The Sydney Symphony was scheduled to begin in five minutes. They settled back for an enjoyable evening.

Jeff and Aaron, like thousands of others, appreciated the beauty and acoustic wonder of the opera house. Approaching from the outside one is struck by the flowing sail like appearance of the whole structure. Nearly everyone has seen the picture in numerous travel stories and magazines. What pictures can not do is replicate looks, feels, and sounds on the inside. The concert hall was the venue for tonight's Symphony concert. It is an acoustic marvel. No microphones are needed. Yet, all two thousand people seated comfortably in elegant cushion seats can hear sounds of the orchestra as well as any vocalists.

"I am always impressed with the sound in here," commented Jeff. "Those suspended plastic donut shaped rings above the stage really do wonders reflecting sound down to the orchestra so that each member can hear themselves. Really remarkable."

"Yes, the sound is always great," replied Aaron; "but, I always like the elegant wood finish and the coordinated coloring of strategically located fabrics which help preserve the pure sound of instruments. You know the opera venue is equally elegant and acoustically tuned for vocal sound. You should try it more often."

Jeff frowned.

"Try it Jeff, opera will expand your cultural horizons."

"I'll accept your professional journalistic reporting of the elegance and sound. Opera is beyond my cultural horizon."

As usual, just about every seat was filled. The lights were blinking for the third and final time..

"Looks sold out," commented Jeff.

"I told you tickets were scarce for this final performance. It looks like nearly all seats are filled. The last seat in our row to your left was just taken."

At that the light dimmed and the conductor entered stage left to a slowly louder round of applause. The concert began. The Beethoven Fifth Symphony was first on the program ending in intermission. The second half of the evening began with a light Chopin string piece followed by the climatic Tschaikovsky 1812 Overture.

At the close of the last encore, the nearly unanimous standing ovation began. Jeff and Aaron were on their feet applauding. They smiled in enjoyment and began to stir about as the lights came up and people began to move down the aisles toward the exits.

"Excuse me," said Jeff as he stepped in front of an elderly gentleman who seemed to have remained seated. As he moved past the gentleman Jeff bumped his knee lightly.

"Excuse me," added Aaron as she moved by the same gentleman, also inadvertently bumping him as she passed in from.

"EEEEKKK."

The scream from behind Jeff and Aaron was enlarged by several "OHs" from other persons behind and around them. They looked back and saw what had caused the commotion. The nicely dressed gentleman who had remained seated during encore ovations had tumbled out of his seat and now lay face down on the floor. His back and the back of the seat he was sitting in were covered with blood. He did not move. There were more screams and people began to move away quickly. Jeff and Aaron stopped and stared.

Aaron reached down and felt his wrist. "Jeff, I think this man is dead."

There were more screams and "ohs" from people in the lower central part of the hall. Quickly two Opera House Security persons were rushing into the hall. They made their way "upstream" through the throng of stunned people.

"What's the problem," asked the first security person.

"This man has been shot, I think he's dead," declared Jeff.

"John, we have a serious problem," said the first security to the second security. "I'll call for police. Try to get the people outside into the foyer."

"Right. Move out into the foyer, please," the security person spoke calmly. He directed people firmly but very politely rather than shouting at them.

Within minutes, which seemed like hours to the stunned people milling around in the foyer, uniformed Sydney police were on the scene. They acted quickly and professionally. They proceeded to secure the center of the hall and asked people to wait in the foyer. One officer asked if anyone had seen or heard what happened.

An elderly, well dressed couple said they were seated two seats down and behind the poor soul. They hadn't seen or heard anything. There were some loud crescendos in the music. Maybe something happened then.

"We saw him out in the lobby at intermission," offered the elderly lady.

"Anyone sitting next to him?" asked the officer.

"We were sitting two seats down from him in the same row," offered Aaron. "In fact, he fell over when I bumped against him when we were leaving."

"Please remain nearby," commanded one of the officers. "Anyone else who was near this person or might have heard something, please remain right here."

Two other officers were setting up a secured area in the lobby where they could talk to people in semiprivacy. Other officers were arriving including plain clothes homicide. One person seemed to be taking charge of the operations. After about fifteen minutes, he approached the still buzzing throng of 100 or so people who were still in the lobby. After some discussion with the Opera House security and the first police officer on the scene he approached Aaron and Jeff.

"Please step over here," he asked them as he pointed to the secured area. "I am lieutenant Wilson." I understand you were the people who discovered the body.

"That's correct," answered Jeff. "We moved past him and each of us bumped him as we passed in front. It seemed strange he didn't get out of his seat."

"I just thought he wanted to let everyone get past before getting out himself," added Aaron. "I just assumed maybe he had difficulty moving and was waiting for the crowd to pass. Then after we had passed in front and were leaving the row someone behind us screamed. We turned around and found the victim had fallen on the floor."

"Did you hear anything during the concert?" asked Wilson. "Like a shot."

"Not a thing," replied Jeff.

"There were moments in the concert when the percussion and brass was loud," added Aaron. "I suppose it could have happened during one of those moments. Especially if someone knew the music and knew precisely when those moments would occur."

"But, I was sitting almost next to him," Jeff continued. "I think I would have heard a shot if it had come from nearby, like just behind him. Is their any evidence that a silencer might have been used?"

"No way to tell for sure. But it was close range. There appear to be powder burns on the back of the seat where the bullet passed through the back of the seat and into his body. Who was seated behind him?" asked Lieutenant Wilson.

"I have no idea," replied Aaron.

"Nor I," added Jeff.

"Lieutenant, I'm Aaron Worthington, Editor with the Sydney Herald," Aaron announced. "I am certain our beat reporters will be calling you. Is there anything you can tell me at this time?"

Wilson's mouth dropped open, taken aback. He had been caught off guard. "This is the first time the press has gotten to me while I am just beginning an investigation. And are you with the Herald also?" he asked turning to Jeff.

"No. I'm Jeff Spencer. But, I am a journalist. I'm a free lance writer."

"Your accent. American or Canadian."

"American. San Francisco. Sometimes Chicago. Sometimes Kansas City."

"Lieutenant, who was the deceased person?" asked Aaron.

"His drivers license says he was Stanley Hutch with an address out in Bondi Beach."

"Did he have anything on him which someone might want?"

"Nothing turned up so far. It did seem that he had a brown envelope in his jacket pocket with a computer disk inside the envelope. We are going to have to investigate."

Aaron made a mental note to get to a phone in the lobby and get a reporter out to his home to see what could be found. She knew tomorrow's page one headlines would read, "MURDER IN THE OPERA HOUSE." They might be able to get a jump on finding information before police controlled the flow of information. Especially if she could get a reporter into the Opera House and into his home in Bondi.

Wilson had been caught off guard by the journalists. He did not want to lose control. He realized he had given more information than he wanted to give. "Look," he commanded, "have your paper's reporters speak to me personally. We'll see what we can do about releasing information." Lieutenant Wilson realized that the pure drama of a murder in the famed opera house was headline stuff. Possibly even page one. Especially if this was a slow news day. Privately he hoped the victim was just an ordinary bloke and the story about his death would be stale and boring news after a couple of days.

# PINE GAP

Pine Gap is a semi secret military base in the desolate arid desert of central Australia. It lies in the Northern Territory just a few miles south and west of the small town of Alice Springs. Few Americans have ever heard of the nearby town, much less the military base. It has been kept pretty much a secret from most Americans. Not many more Australians are aware of the base. It isn't a totally secret base, though. Many of the 25,000 residents of Alice Springs know there are some military personnel outside of town in the desert behind the hills. There is a bitumen hard road turning off the Alice Springs to Adelaide Highway. It is sealed all ten miles up to the main gates. No civilians are allowed through the gates. But, the military personnel shop in town. Some live in town, some live on the base. Those who live in town are part of the local community. They coach softball teams, lawn bowl at the local club, play golf. Some of the wives work in the stores, teach in the school, and work at the Flying Doctor Hospital. Australian and American military personnel work and live side by side at the base and in the town of Alice Springs. Pine Gap is not a "secret base" in the sense of Soviet secret bases in Siberia or even United States secret bases in the Nevada desert.

What goes on at the base is still highly secret. Locals know it has something to do with cold war satellite reconnaissance. Since the end of the cold war, there were trouble spots all over the world. Satellite based intelligence is still as important as it ever was. The work of the men and women at the base never ceased.

The base was located where it was, in the middle of the desolate outback half way around the world from major hot spots for good reason. It was easy to keep secure. There was no nosy press. Few people knew about the place. It would be easy to defend if that ever became necessary.

Most of the tourists in and out of the town of Alice Springs noticed the entrance to the base. Tourists would see the entrance on their way into Alice to take camel or four wheel drive safaris into the outback desert. Their safaris usually bypassed the base.

Pine Gap was a joint operation between the United States and Australia because of the many joint interests of the two nations in so many potentially trouble spots in the modern world. Both had strong vested interests in stability throughout the Pacific Rim and all of Asia. They both had long historical links and interests with Europe.

There had been numerous trouble spots in Asia since World War II which had usually been of common concern to both the Australians and the Americans. Korea and Vietnam were obvious. Indonesia and the Philippines was a concern. Australia worried about troubles in East Timor. Unrest in the jungles of Indonesia and Malaysia were of concern.

On this Tuesday at the Pine Gap base, Major Frank Everhart (Royal Australian Air Force) and Major Janetta Jackson (United States Air Force) were reviewing communications for the last month between the base and other United States bases operating around the world.

"Frank, have you seen some unusual activity in some of the data bases?" asked Jackson.

"I saw three unusual sign - ons about a month ago," Everhart replied. "Have you found something more?"

"Yes. I note three—no—four sign—ons this month. These don't appear to be from any known source. They must be 'bastards'." Bastard was a military slang term for illegal or unauthorized entries into computer systems.

"I think we need to report this to DP Security," commented Jackson.

"I agree," echoed Everhart. He reached for a phone and pushed one button. In less than three seconds he was speaking. "Colonel, this is Major Everhart. Major Jackson and I have been conducting a routine review of communications. We have noticed some 'bastards'. I think they should be investigated. There may have been a breech of security. It may be just some kids hacking away. Then, again, it may be something serious."

25

Replacing the phone, he looked at Jackson and commented, "We've covered our rears. If its kids hacking, DP security will find it and scare the BeeGees out of them. If its more serious, we may have stopped something serious."

"Frank, here is another suspicious sign - on this week. It doesn't look right to me."

The security buzzer went off announcing the entry of another person into the workroom. Only a person with a specified security clearance was allowed to enter the room. Anyone entering set off a warning buzzer and was photographed automatically as they came through the door. Captain Germain McGregor, U.S. Air Force DP Security Specialist entered the room.

"Frank, Janetta," he addressed his superiors without reference to rank. They worked on so many projects together so often, a casualness of communication was normal. It was also a consequence of the Aussie military placing less importance on ranks separating people. They tended to see it as a barrier to getting the job done, whatever the job might be. "You have found a problem?"

"We aren't sure how much of a problem it is," replied Janetta. "But, we have noticed several 'bastard' sign-ons."

"At least four this month and at least three last month. We though it should be checked out. Probably just some smart bored kids hacking away in Sydney."

"Right. Can you bring up the logs and give me a hard copy? I'll take it from there."

So far the matter seemed almost routine. This sort of thing happened more frequently now that more people had access to computer technology in their homes. There had been a few incidents of Soviet and Israeli security forces trying to enter the secured communication data flow and even data bases. They had been identified quickly and closed. Then there had been some efforts by India and Pakistan to try to find out information about each other through U.S. and Australia communications. That had been closed.

For about three years there had been increasing incidents of nuisance 'hacking' mostly by teen age kids in Australia and even in the United States looking for something challenging to do rather than doing boring school homework. Actually, the kid hackers were often the best. They were more innovative and less structured in their thinking. Thus, they were successful at cracking security codes. The kids thrived on it. They seemed to get sheer delight out of just beating the system. For those who succeeded, it was like a badge of honor among their 'nerdy' friends.

The kids and the secret agents all annoyed the top brass. They had to be concerned. It might take only one serious breech of security at the wrong time to create havoc. Consequently, they insisted that all security breeches by closely monitored and investigated.

There was always some kind of secret operation being planned or actually in progress. Any kind of threat to the security of those operations had to be taken very seriously.

# WESTERN KANSAS

Western central Kansas is wheat country. Miles and miles of wheat. In early spring the wheat is growing rapidly in the warm days and cool nights. No scorching heat yet. That will come nearer to harvest time.

Farmers in Kansas depend upon a good wheat crop. The millions of bushels come from single stalks of wheat which have a growing head full of grain. Dozens of grains from each stalk combined with billions of stalks produce tons and tons of grain.

Towns like Emden have long depended upon the income from wheat farmers for their existence. Grain elevators have supported truckers who have supported service businesses which supported stores all of which supported banks and commodity dealers. Wheat was life to Emden. It had been like that ever since the German settlers arrived in the 1870's. They brought with them their centuries old Red Turkish strain of wheat which was still the base of today's high grade hybrid seeds. The land produced good wheat except when there were bad years. Like the dust bowl days of the 1930's. Then the wheat crops died. Some of the towns died. Most towns were stunned. A few hearty towns survived. As later improvements in seed, financing, marketing, and exports came, the surviving towns resurged. Today, Emden having survived the ups and downs was a thriving rural Kansas wheat farming center.

The town of Emden is supported by large farms. Most farms are at least 600 acres. A section of land. The majority of farm operators were still family farmers owning part of what they farmed and contracting to farm more land. If they worked hard, were fortunate to have good weather, and got a break on world market prices, they did well.

Delbert Kettering was standing in the middle of one of his large tracts of wheat. He, along with Rachael and his two teen age sons farmed 1200 acres of Kansas wheat land. Naturally, they grew mostly wheat. Between them and their hired hands

28

there were eight families directly dependent upon the success of the wheat crop each year.

Kettering was frowning. He was seeing it again. He knew the signs of every insect and germ which might have an impact on the success of his crop. He had never seen this kind of rust forming this early on the crop. It wasn't all over, but it was popping up in several fields. He was puzzled and had a nagging concern. He had heard rumors of some new strain of rust appearing in the next county west. He made a decision. He reached down and plucked a plant which was just beginning to show rust. He carefully pulled the entire plant and root. He walked about fifty feet and found another area of rust. He plucked another plant. He repeated the behavior ten times over the area of about 100 acres. He was going to take the ten samples to the University of Kansas Agricultural Research lab in Lawrence. He could take it into a branch office in Emden; but, he wanted to avoid delay. If this was anything serious, he didn't want to waste any time finding out what could be done.

As Kettering walked through the back door into the kitchen of his Kansas home, his wife Rachael was working in the spare room they used as an office. Their farm operation was truly a partnership. Rachael had a business degree from the University of Kansas. She was a natural for the business side of the farming operation. She kept the records, handled taxes, and coordinated much of their planning. She had the entire farm operation computerized. All record keeping was kept in spreadsheet files which were easily transferable to the tax preparation documents. Rachael and Delbert filed their farm operation tax returns electronically. Rachael had complete records of each field they farmed. She had complete records including seeding, fertilizer and insecticides, and yields for the last fifteen years. Her data bases included crop damages for a variety of reasons. Given less than five minutes to access files she could tell you the complete productivity record of any 50 acres tract of land they farmed. Further, she had market price data history for each day of each year for fifteen years by location; i.e. local markets, national markets, futures. She even had a data base on world markets. She could access through the internet a huge volume of current world production and market information made available from the University of Kansas Agricultural Extension Service in Lawrence, Kansas.

"Del, I'm in the office working on market data analysis," Rachael called.

Delbert walked into the office and went straight to the bookshelves. He reached for his latest plant agronomy book. Then he reached for his botany book. "Racheal, something is troubling me about our wheat crop." Delbert had that half puzzled, half worried look on his face. "I found some rust on a few plants. Do you remember that alert last week on the crop report from AGSERV?" he asked.

"I don't recall," Rachael replied.

"It was a short item on some strange rust problems in Colben County. Seemed to be something which spread rapidly. Something about no explanation. Fields had to be plowed under."

"Why?"

"I found some strange rust. It may be the same thing. I've looked through everything in this book and its the latest edition. I didn't find a thing matching this rust which is beginning to appear."

By the time Delbert had finished looking through everything in his latest books, Rachael had signed onto the internet and was searching the UNIVERSE index for any cross listing of 'rust', 'unexplained', and 'recent'. "Del, I've got three entries. Look."

Delbert and Rachael both watched the screen as she listed all three and then systematically located each and downloaded the short report descriptions.

"First one is the report I saw last week," Delbert commented. "It was in Colben county. Nothing identified."

"The second one is the analysis report filed by the University of Kansas with the U.S. Department of Agriculture," Rachael read form the screen. "Rust seems to strangle the cells by blocking waste elimination. The blocking seems to be from processes unidentifiable."

"But, rust usually kills plants by injecting a poison protein into the plant," Delbert commented. "This is some new kind of rust."

"The third report is filed from Darling Downs region of Queensland Australia," Rachael read. "That report is six months old but there is no follow-up report. I'm not sure that will be helpful to us."

"Listen Racheal, I'm really concerned about our wheat field. If this begins to spread and we don't have some way to respond, it could devastate our yields this year."

"What do you have in mind?"

"I am going to take these sample plants straight to Lawrence to the University Lab. Hopefully someone there can help us."

"Won't it take days or even weeks even if they begin analysis immediately? It may not be a high priority item with them?"

"Can't wait. They have to understand it isn't just us. If our crop is infected, it means the spores causing the rust are airborne. Look how rapidly they must have spread from Colben County. It will have to become a high priority item."

"Right, the rapid spreading means they are carried by prevailing winds."

"It will take me about three hours to drive to Lawrence and get to the Lab. I have met Dr. Wilson Blaine who is in charge of the research lab. We met at a plant seminar last year in Abilene. I hope to get to him and urge him to place an immediate rush on this analysis."

"Del, it will take you more like four hours to make that drive. While you are on the way, let me do some connecting. I'll get on the internet superhighway and have them waiting for you at Dr. Wilson's lab in Lawrence. I'll connect with County Extension, the Governor's Office for Agricultural Support, State Senator Hopper's office in Topeka. I'll bet I can get things

*George E. Tuttle*

happening faster on the information superhighway than you can driving from here to Lawrence."

"No kidding," Del replied with a smile. "If you can get any or all of our influential contacts to alert Lawrence, we might be able to head off a serious disaster. We need the university and government researchers to get on this problem pronto."

# NORTH RYDE

Ngarrie Bhojammie, better know to his friend as 'N.B.' was checking inventory in the plant lab at Macquarie University. Macquarie University was a modern metropolitan university located in North Ryde, a newer upscale suburb of Sydney, Australia. The university had recently been expanded under the plan to reorganize higher education in Australia. It's highly regarded record of success in the arts, business, and humanities had caused the national powers that be in higher education to hand it the mission to establish national and international prominence in basic sciences. That mission had led to establishing several doctoral programs and accompanying research labs in several of the sciences. One of those areas was plant agronomy. Dr. Nigel Harrington had studied in both England and the United States. He was attracted to Macquarie to develop his specialty, plant agronomy which brought together the scientific study of plants with the broader study of field management.

Plant agronomy was extremely important to agriculture all along the eastern coast of Australia from Melbourne in the south to the Atherton tablelands west of Cairns in the north. That meant everything from tropical plants to grains, to vineyards, to forest and grasses.

Dr. Harrington had attracted a loyal cadre of faculty and ambitious students. One of the ambitious students was Ngarrie 'Art' Bhojammie. Bhojammie was an atypical doctoral student. He was one of a handful of native aboriginals who had successfully pursued graduate education. There had been a few before him. Mostly they had pursued programs in the arts and law. Two individuals had become successful as zoologists. 'N.B.' was the first aboriginal doctoral student in plant agronomy.

It was difficult for aboriginal students to overcome the cultural challenge to pursuing white man's formal education. Once a few crossed over that cultural barrier, they needed monetary and mentoring support to succeed. It was usually easier to pursue paths in arts and law and animal sciences. The easiest path to follow was the one closest to what the aboriginal could draw upon from his thousands of years of ancestral culture. That was animals. The native aboriginal had a cultural interest in animals. Their mythology recognized the great lizard or the great crocodile. N.B. took the hard road. Aboriginals have seldom become 'gatherers' or 'tillers of the soil.' Plant agronomy was totally foreign. But, N.B. had an unusual interest in plants and crops. He was a good doctoral student working with Dr. Harrington.

Harrington had initially been reluctant to accept and work with Bhojammie. He knew the disadvantages. It was during an entrance interview that Harrington was struck by Ngarrie's determination. His credentials were superb. Harrington had accepted Ngarrie's application and supported it for government funded research. Over the course of two years Bhojammie and Harrington had progressed from student and teacher to cooperating researchers. They had several joint projects which had resulted in important research reports for the government and for private seed companies in Australia. They had even shared research findings with United States researchers at a recent world conference.

Ngarrie completed the inventory he was working on and studied the sheet with a puzzled look. Something was missing. He headed for Dr. Harrington's office.

"Nigel, we are missing some plant cell samples," reported Ngarrie. Dr. Harrington insisted on his doctoral students being on a first name basis with him. After all this was the land of 'mates' and casualness.

"Probably those samples we sent to Canberra. They contained some analysis of unique wheat cell growth from Garra Garra up in Darling Downs in Queensland," replied Harrington.

"But they are still on our inventory." Ngarrie looked puzzled.

"They went out yesterday afternoon by courier. I suspect the dispatch form is still on the secretary's desk. If so, it hasn't been removed from inventory. Check with Karen."

Ngarrie turned and walked from the lab into a small office crowded with file cabinets, computers terminals, and boxes of supplies. He approached Karen Simpson's desk.

"Karen, do you have any forms for some sample bottles picked up by a courier yesterday?" he asked.

"They should be in the top file. Any problem?"

"No problem now. I need to record the dispatch form on the inventory record. You know how things can get lost around an academic office."

"I try. There 'IS' only one of me."

"I know, you do the work of three. No worries. Would you like a tea?" Years ago Ngarrie had acquired the Aussie custom of 'tea' at mid morning and mid afternoon. Unlike tea in England it did not necessarily mean tea. 'Tea' had become a popular phrase better known in the United States as 'break time.' For Ngarrie 'tea' usually meant a coke.

"N.B., make my 'tea' the same as yours."

"Diet or classic?"

"Classic. I need the caffeine. This report to the curriculum committee was due yesterday. I am going to have to have my 'tea' as I work."

"No way," replied Ngarrie. "Now be a good Aussie. Stop what you are doing. Here's your classic. Let's go catch some fresh air out on the quad."

"OK, you convinced me. I'll be a good Aussie."

It is an unwritten rule in Australia that 'tea time' is an obligatory ritual. It would be deemed unpatriotic to pass up 'tea time.' Therefore, N.B. and Karen joined several other staff on a small courtyard patio for 'tea.'

# BONDI BEACH

Lt. Ed Wilson and two other Sydney Metro police officers were looking carefully through the house at Bondi Beach. They had obtained the address for Stanley Hutch from the Bureau of Records after interviewing many of the patrons of the Opera House who had been seated near Hatch when he was killed.

The house Stanley had lived in was a small cottage type, like many others in the Bondi Beach area. It had two bedrooms, a small living room, a small dining room, a small but functional kitchen. At some point someone had finished another room in the upstairs. It was not used by Hutch except for storage. The outside was neatly painted light blue with white trim. Gingerbread along the facia was in good condition. The house had been kept nicely inside. There was a hall closet as well as a small closet in each of the two bedrooms. The kitchen had a pantry with canned and packaged goods filling most of the shelves. Hutch ate a lot of canned and prepared goods. His refrigerator contained a six pack of Foster's beer, milk, bread, some cheese, some packaged meats.

The police determined he had a distant niece in Broome on the far northwest coast. As far as anyone could tell she was the only living next of kin. They had contacted police in Western Australia who would arrange for police in Broome to contact his niece. Today they were beginning the search of his small home in Bondi. Hopefully they would find some clue to who killed him and why he was killed.

The police knew virtually nothing about the man. A few of the people at the Opera House remembered seeing him at other concerts. Two of the Opera House staff recognized him as a somewhat regular. He attended two or three times a month. Sometimes he was around at other free performances at the Opera House. The neighbors in Bondi Beach knew he came and went regularly. However, no one knew much about him. He had seemed a pleasant man, but a loner. The bottom line was that no one at the Opera House or his neighbors knew much about him. He was a mystery.

The police started looking in the living room. They didn't know what they were looking for. Some scrap of paper. A letter. A piece of mail. Anything. Nothing in his small living room. Nothing in the kitchen. They were going through his bedroom.

"Lieutenant, this guy wasn't quirky. No girlie magazines. No junkie mail."

"Hey. Look here on these shelves. Looks like a stack of some sort of programs. They're opera and symphony programs. And beside them is a box with ticket stubs. Must be dozens. This guy spent a lot of time at the Opera House."

"Figures. That's where he was killed. And, he was recognized by people there."

"Looks like he played the horses too," announced Wilson as he looked through the top drawer of the small desk in the bedroom. "Here's a pile of stubs. Doesn't look like he was a big enough winner to constitute a candidate for cheating on his taxes. But, he played regularly."

One of the policemen asked, "what was on the computer disk found in his pocket at the Opera House, lieutenant?"

"We don't know yet. Someone from the lab is trying to access whatever is on the disk. Could be anything. We'll have that report soon."

"Lieutenant, over here in the back of his closet. There is some sort of pouch."

"Pick it up carefully. Sealed?"

"Locked, like one of those courier pouches."

"No key."

"No but, I can probably pick this baby. OK Lieutenant?"

"Yea, go ahead. If we were trying to make a case against him we would have to be concerned about breaking into that pouch. We would need a warrant to even be here much less open his locked pouch. But, he's dead. We're trying to find clues to who and why."

"It's a snap Lieutenant. Look's like some bottles. There's some paper here."

"Great, let me see the paper." Wilson read the paper quickly. "Looks like some kind of delivery to be made in Canberra. It seems to have come from some lab at Macquarie University. May be important. Let's take it back. For now, let's keep looking."

The three police officers continued going through every box, every book, under mattresses, into every closet. They found some check stubs and paid bills. The bank account could be checked for any unusual activity. They found nothing more.

The police did not happen to notice the nondescript blue car setting parked in the next block from Stanley Hutch's home. The two occupants of the blue car sat hunched down watching the police as they went in and out of the house. The car remained there until the last evidence of the police disappeared.

# ST. LEONARDS

Frank Bengotti was just completing his order for more plants. He placed the order over the internet connection to the island of Halmarhera in North Maluka Province of Indonesia. He knew the order would be relayed to farmers among the seldom seen native tribes in the mountain jungle region of Halmahera Indonesia. As he was signing off he reached to click off when he noticed a blip on the screen. Immediately he realized that it was a recently installed security system to recognize and notify the user of any unauthorized effort to break the system security.

"Al, come here," Frank called to his brother, Al, working across the room. "We just had someone trying to break into our system."

"Did they bust in?" asked Al.

"Damn, I don't know. You know I don't know anything about this high tech gadget. That's why we hired Lassiter. Get Lassiter in here to check out the system."

Harrold Lassiter was ex military communications who had made himself into a computer expert. His expertise was for hire to the best bidder. Bengottis needed someone with Harrold's expertise to set up and sustain the communications of their operation. The key was to maintain secrecy of their suppliers in Indonesia and to maintain fast network communications throughout Australia. Like any other company utilizing state of the art computer systems, they were vulnerable to any number of 'hackers' who might make it into their system. Smart ass teenagers were a pain. There was always some kid making it in. They were more concerned about market competitors, like the Wuan enterprises, succeeding in breaking their security.

Harrold Lassiter spent a lot of time tracing the breaks and re-securing the system. When he located a teen age 'hacker' he left it to Bengottis enforcers to persuade the errant teen not to do that again. Usually, it was enough to enter the home late at night, smash the equipment, and leave a note suggesting what the teen should not do in the future. It always worked. He or she never complained to the police.

Al rushed out and caught Lassiter about to go home for the day. He hurried him into the main office.

"Harrold, we got another 'hacker' trying to get in," announced Frank Bengotti. "Find him and we'll send some boys to scare the gee-gees out of him."

Lassiter sat down at the terminal and after about two minutes of working his magic on the keys he announced tersely, "He got in and it isn't any teen age kid."

There was stunned silence. Frank looked at Al. Al looked at Frank. They both looked at Lassiter and jointly exclaimed "How?"

"It will take me a while to figure out how and how much data they got. Order me some pizza. I'm going to be a while."

Frank turned to Al. "Have Tracie order a lot of pizza. None of us is going anywhere until we find out how badly we been hit and what we can do about it."

"All I can say at this point is that this is no kid. Whoever it is has been in more than once and we have definitely been hit. And worse, I got a hunch some data has been massaged."

"What do you mean, massaged?"

"I mean someone has been going in an changing some of our data."

"Why."

"Who knows. Maybe they want to disrupt our distribution system. Maybe they want to foul up our orders so we get over stocked and bogged down with too much  inventory in the pipeline. Maybe they want to scramble our past records so that our long range projections are all screwed up. Who knows!"

The two Bengotti brothers sank dejectedly into chairs. They did not have to speak. Their dejected expressions were already saying what they thought. They knew that somehow the Wuans were behind this effort to hack into their data bases.

# SYDNEY

Jeff Spencer was sitting in his corner room at the Park Regis Hotel on the twelfth floor. He was sitting at the large window overlooking William Street as it runs east toward Hyde Park across and on to Kings Cross and across Elizabeth Street as it runs north toward the Opera House. It was a beautiful sunny morning. He had just finished his muffin, cereal, juice, and coffee. No need for room service. He had grabbed what he needed at Woolworth's food department a block west above the metro tube station. Between his fridge and the hot pot he could fix all he wanted for breakfast.

He was seated at the table in front of the window watching the people scurrying below across Hyde Park in all directions. He had his computer and modem handy to begin work. The morning Sydney Herald was sprawled in the chair next to his table. The television was on. In the background he heard the morning ABC news team describing the latest political mud slinging in Canberra. He thought, no different than in the United States.

Jeff was being drawn more and more to his lap top. He was checking some news service stories from both domestic and foreign Australian sources. There were more upbeat news items on the service lines than ever made it onto the daily newscast. Also just like home.

He was struck by an item filed by a local reporter out of Toowoomba. Toowoomba was west of Brisbane on the edge of the Darling Downs agriculture region. Few people outside of Australia realized the significance of the region to Australia and to the world's food supply. Most people envision most of interior Australia as nothing but desert and barren land. Several regions lying no more than two to three hundred miles inland are very fine agricultural growing regions. The Atherton Tablelands west of Cairns is such a region. Another is the dry but rich irrigated wheat land east of Perth. Gippsland and the region east and northeast of Melbourne is another. The Murray valley north of Melbourne and the region north of the Murray valley are fine wine regions. The Barossa Valley northeast of Adelaide is also fine wine country.

The Darling Downs was perhaps the finest growing region outside of central United States and the San Jaoquin Valley of California. Toowoomba was the closest town of any size to the Downs. It was from Toowoomba that a news story had been filed which caught Jeff's interest.

Jeff's interest was caught by the lead line "Downs Wheat Farmers Saved." He read the rest of the story. It turned out to be more than a paragraph. Actually it was more feature story length. The story claimed that the long drought in the Downs region, which had plagued much of Australia, was broken one year ago leading to a bumper crop of wheat. The story read: "Just when farmers thought they had turned the corner, a strain of plant rust has developed this year. Extensive plant pathology research at Macquarie University and the Australian Federal Research Center in southwestern Queensland had located the cause of the problem and developed a treatment just in time to salvage about seventy-percent of this year's crop. The current research was going on to develop a soil innoculation process to be applied this coming fall to assure that subsequent rust would not return during the second year."

It looked like a good positive kind of story. He would file it away and index it for some future use as an interesting filler to fit with the right story.

Jeff's attention was captured by the television headline coming from the set he had been ignoring. "Police are baffled by the recent Opera House Murder." He turned and saw an ABC reporter standing in front of the Opera House.

The reporter was asking the police Lieutenant about the case. "Lieutenant, is it true you don't have any leads yet in the murder last night in the Opera House?"

"We don't have a firm suspect at this time; but, we are pursuing several interesting clues."

"Is it true that two people have called in confessing to the crime?"

"We always have some incidents in a case like this where someone—a little unbalanced—wants to get attention and claims they committed a crime. We had one such call from a party whose voice we recognized. That same person has called and claimed they committed each of the last ten murders in New South Wales."

"Could that be a serial killer, Lieutenant?"

"No. The individual making those calls is calling from a pay phone inside the New South Wales State Prison. We know who it is and that person has been behind bars for the last five years. That person is presently safely locked away."

"Is it true that Aaron Worthington, an editor from the Sydney Herald was at the scene of the murder?"

"Ms Worthington was seated near the victim."

"Lieutenant, has she been able to offer any clues? Did she see the crime committed?"

"You need to talk to Ms. Worthington about what she saw or knows. Sorry, I can't give you any more than that."

"Ladies and gentlemen, ABC News has learned that Sydney Herald Editor, Aaron Worthington, who was seated near the murder victim has been meeting with police and may have provided clues to solving this case. Ms. Worthington is well known for her journalistic record which has helped solve several mysterious murders and robberies in Australia during the last five years. Now back to our studio."

A soap commercial suddenly appeared on the screen.

At that very moment, the phone rang that distinctive double ringing sound typical of the telephones in Australia. Jeff picked up the receiver and said: "Spencer here."

"Jeff did you see that lousy Anderson from ABC? He is telling the world that I know something about the murder. Damn him."

"Well, you and I were there when he was found. Do you know anything?"

43

"Jeff. Not you too? You know better than to believe what some wet behind the ears young puppy faced rookie reporter makes up as news."

"You mean you don't know anything?"

"Of course not. Jeff, meet me in ten minutes at the 1-2-3 Cafe, out on the balcony where we can talk. By."

The phone was dead. Aaron was definitely upset. She was more upset than just having her name on television again. He decided he had better close down his computer and dash downstairs. He could just make it to the 1-2-3 Cafe in ten minutes. Something was certainly upsetting Aaron.

Jeff walked quickly down Pitt street as the Sydney Monorail hummed quietly overhead on the other side of the street. Jeff was distracted by the humming monorail as it glided along. He thought it amazing that in just a few short years the monorail was constructed linking the vibrant downtown of Sydney with a newly reconstructed Darling Harbor about a mile to the south. The new Darling Harbor replaced rows of decaying old warehouses left over from the nineteenth century. The vibrant changing downtown, the new Darling Harbor, and the state of the art high tech monorail demonstrated that Sydney was one of the vibrant cities in the world.

As he stepped into the Pitt Street Mall his thoughts returned to the urgency of Aaron's phone call. He could see the outside balcony of the 1-2-3 Cafe just a few feet ahead. He hurried into the building, up the open circular stairway two steps at a time. Arriving at the 1-2-3 Cafe door on the second floor he could see Aaron already seated outside on the balcony in a secluded corner behind a live potted plant and overlooking the Strand Mall below. Jeff nodded to the hostess and hurried on through.

"Aaron, what's up? You sounded upset. You don't like being caught on television news camera?"

"NO! I don't. But that is not what's bothering me. Jeff, the police are putting a lid on this murder case."

"How do you know?"

"Jeff, knowing what's going on in this city is my business. I'm a journalist."

"So, what's going on."

"Jeff, don't be patronizing. I know because we have a news intern who was riding in on the bus from Bondi and saw the police swarming around a house. Being an aggressive reporter, she got off the bus and investigated."

"You mean she talked to the police?"

"Hell no! She hung around the bushes outside and overheard some conversation. Jeff, it was the home of that poor fellow who was murdered at the Opera House. They have some clues, but they have a lid on the case."

"How do you know?"

"Later, she went down to police headquarters and tried to get access to what was going on. She was told they know nothing more than they did last night."

"How did the ABC television get wind of a story? They even had your name."

"I'm not sure. But, that isn't important. There is something which makes this more than just a murder of a poor middle aged man at the Opera House."

"How do you know?"

"I sense it, damn it. I know the police have information. They are trying to keep everything quiet. That makes me suspicious."

"Sound's like you are going to become involved in solving another mysterious case. The last one was a murder too."

"Become involved? Please. I'm already involved. It happened right next to us."

"It was a few seats away."

"Same thing. I'm involved. You're involved. I have a feeling this is not a simple case."

"Sooo. You're going to do what?" asked Jeff.

"For now, two things. First, the official story. I am having that intern, Jennifer Cross, pursue the official investigation as a possible news story for the Herald. She's young, smart, aggressive, and hungry for success as a journalist. She will follow all of the angles with the police, his neighbors, his house if she can get past the police."

"You think she has enough experience to get much?"

"I'm feeding her suggestions via her e-mail. She's smart and she's eager to succeed."

"And what's the second thing you are going to do? I have a feeling it isn't 'official.'"

"I am going to find out where he worked, what he did, who he banked with. Anything I can find. I want to know what happened, why, and who was involved. There may be a big story here. If not, at least I might be able to help the police."

"Are you sure they want your help? The cases you have been involved in have turned out well, but the police have not seemed to appreciate your efforts."

"They're jealous. In the jewel robbery at the state museum they had no leads. I did their work for them because I was a private citizen and I could ask questions, do things the police could not do without a warrant or alerting people they were under investigation. Same thing with that robbery of the National Library in Canberra. Same thing with that last murder at General Foods Corporate headquarters in North Sydney. Are you with me on this one?"

"I guess so. What good would it do to say no. I said no on the last two cases, but I got involved anyway. I know how consuming this will become to you. If I want to see anything of you while I'm in Sydney, I guess I'll need to string along."

"Ok; but you don't have to do this."

"Yes I do. However, I do have to also get my own investigations done and file my own stories back to San Francisco. That's how I make money. But, I'll do what I can."

"Great. Now, here's my plan. I'm going back to my office and begin checking every data base I can think of. When I find where he worked, I'll give you a call. Join me if you can."

Aaron folded her napkin, picked up the bill, gave Jeff a quick kiss, and dashed out stopping briefly to pay the bill. Jeff sat on the balcony finishing his coffee watching her exit the building, cross the Pitt Street  mall, enter the Strand building to go through and back to the Sydney Herald building on the other side of George Street. He wondered where this escapade was going to take him. Where it was going to take them.

# LAWRENCE, KANSAS

Del Kettering was waiting in the office of Dr. Wilson Blaine at the Plant Research Lab on the campus of the University of Kansas in Lawrence, Kansas. His trip had been an uneventful drive to Lawrence. He made it in four hours. He had been waiting fifteen minutes for Dr. Blaine.

A secretary said, "Mr. Kettering, Dr. Blaine can see you now."

"Thank you. First office?"

"He'll be in the first door on the left."

"Thank you." Del stepped quickly into the office.

"Mr. Kettering." Dr. Blaine spoke immediately as Del entered the room. "I'm Wilson Blaine. Pleased to meet you. I think we may have crossed paths at the Plains Wheat Conference last year."

"Yes, we did. I didn't think you would remember," replied Kettering.

"You certainly can move fast. I just got off the phone with the Governor's Office. I understand you may have some new wheat plant problem. We'll certainly do all we can to help. But, how do you get the word around so fast while you are driving on the Interstate?"

"My wife, Rachael. She is very competent with the computer. She was going to communicate with everyone she could while I made the drive over here. I am not certain who all she has been able to reach during the last four hours."

"She has been quite successful from what I can tell. At least I know she has been in touch with the State Agriculture Department, the Governor's Office, as well as my office. Actually, her information about other cases of strange rust obtained from the internet give us a more pointed focus to our problem than usually happens. She must be quite skilled."

"She is," replied Del. "A farmer can't make it today without information from other farmers and the best sources possible. She gets that information."

"I hope you have some samples, " replied Dr. Blaine. "We are already hearing about some rust on the Colorado and Kansas state line. If you have some samples we can get them under a scope and hopefully know what's happening."

"Yes," replied Del reaching into the case he was carrying. "I have several collected this morning. I've packed them with moisture to preserve their condition. I hope you can find something. Rachael said there was an article about some similar situation in the county west of us."

"Correct. Her information let me get in touch with the plant specialist for Dexall Seeds lab in Corben, Kansas. It seems he was approached by a farmer who had purchased seed from them thinking he might have had some infected seeds. They can run some test and get the results to me by tomorrow. Their tests will confirm or reject the hypothesis that the seeds were infected in any way. In the mean time I can begin some preliminary microscopic analysis of your samples. We will proceed on the assumption that the infected seed hypothesis can be rejected."

Dr. Blaine had taken the carefully wrapped samples and opened them up. He was transferring them to some specially designed environmentally controlled cases for storage.

Del was pointing to the rust appearing on the short plant stems. "See there, Dr. Blaine, that plant is much too small already to be showing rust."

"Certainly is earlier than normal rust. Usually we catch rust too late in the growing process to have much time to arrest the spread. We may be lucky in this instance by catching it so early. There is an outside chance we can do something to save most of your crop. These are still young plants. The basic growth cells are still functional. At this point they are still quite resilient."

"And maybe stop the spread of the rust to counties further east," added Del. "Dr., what about the internet entry Rachael found in Darling Downs, Australia? Is that a worthwhile lead?"

49

"It may be," replied Blaine. "It's nighttime down under and I can't raise anyone there. But, I've checked the entry Racheal found. I have an e-mail off to the Australian Ministry of Agriculture in Canberra asking for more information. I hope to have a reply tonight. I am going to stay right on this problem. I'll be working here tonight. If there is a reply and they can shed any useful light, I'll know. But, I wouldn't think that will produce much of a result."

"Don't rule it out Dr. Blaine. You know very well the seed companies are international corporations now. They may be testing and growing seed all over the world. What if seeds were grown here and taken there? Our viruses become their viruses. And vice versa."

"Possible, but not likely," replied Blaine. "There are two governmental inspection bodies involved."

"Yea, and both are probably understaffed. Don't rule it out Doctor."

Dr. Blaine nodded agreement.

"Doctor, I'm driving back home. You know how to reach Rachael on the internet. Please keep us informed."

"I certainly will. Hopefully, I can have an update to Rachael by the time you make it home."

# PINE GAP

Captain Germain McGregor, the United States Air Force Security Specialist stationed at Pine Gap Military Base in Australia, had been working for several hours tracing the located security breeches which Majors Everhart and Jackson had asked him to investigate. He was clearly irritated by what he was finding. Usually when he checked out a problem he could quickly find the problem was one of two kinds.

Sometimes equipment was interrupted by something like sunspots which were so powerful their rays created repeated transmission glitches. Usually checking mechanisms filtered out the effects. Once in a great while a glitch got through the various security points and registered as a breech. These occasional instances were identifiable by the magnitude of the wavelength which registered on automatic logging data. It took a little time, but he always found those sources of problems.

More often, some bright, bored, smart assed kid was surfing the world's internet looking for mischief. McGregor knew the type. He had been one. He had grown up on the north side of St. Louis without much to do except 'hang out.' 'Hanging out' was boring. It was also dangerous. People he knew had older brothers who had been hanging out and soon they were in jail or dead. Early on he had decided he did not want to be either one of those. McGregor was fortunate to stumble on a youth education program sponsored by the Washington University and the City of St. Louis. He started out playing chess. One day he found a computer. He watched as the University students recorded their chess scores. At that point he was hooked for life. Ten years later he was a computer genius and happily signed up with the United States Air Force.

But, he was not looking at the work of a bright, bored, smart assed kid. They didn't really mean any harm. They got in once or twice and got out. He could trace them. The Joint Australian\United States Command at Pine Gap decided world security did not require harassing and jailing bright, bored, smart assed kids. Better to identify them, watch them, and bring them into the military. Today's military needed bright high tech people. No, this was not a teenage hacker. There were too many entries. They came from places which were not where some teenage kid was working. These were intentional security violations.

As McGregor was hissing out another, 'Damn Him,' Majors Everhart and Jackson entered the room with drinks and pizza.

"Germain, you need some energy," declared Jackson as she handed him a slice of pizza and a coke. "How is it going?"

There was a long ten second silence while majors Everhart and Jackson looked back and forth at each other. Finally, Captain McGregor spoke softly and very slowly. "We have been violated."

Everhart looked at Jackson and then at McGregor. "You mean someone other than a smart assed kid has broken in?"

"We have been violated by a serious, intentional breach of security. It has happened at least eight times during the last four weeks."

"Where is it coming from?" asked Jackson.

"Four times from somewhere near Sydney and four times from somewhere near Singapore. It looks like the work of the same person. The breech is made the same way each time. He or she must be moving between Sydney and Borneo."

"So what is our action?" asked Everhart.

"We turn this over to joint military intelligence immediately," replied Jackson. "There are joint Australian, British, Indonesian, and American anti terrorist exercises about to begin. Those operations could be compromised. We need to know what is going on here before those exercises begin. They have been too long in the delicate planning stage to have them compromised now."

# NORTH RYDE

Ngarrie Bhojammie had returned from his 'tea' coke break. He sat staring at his computer terminal with a puzzled look on his face. He had checked his E-mail and didn't find what he expected. There was all sorts of incoming mail from all over the world. He had mail from England, France, United States, Argentina, Ukraine and from many locations in Australia. What he was expecting was a confirmation from the National Agricultural Research and Repository Center (NARRC) that they had received the live samples which had been sent to Canberra for recording.

Ngarrie had analyzed wheat samples which had arrived the past week from the Toowoomba and the Darling Downs region of Queensland. There had been an early epidemic of wheat stem rust in the Darling Downs at the beginning of the growing season. Laboratory analysis had suggested a systemic problem which might be corrected in one of four ways. Site experiments had been performed. Now as the harvests season approached it was desired to make post tests on the prevalence of the organism responsible for the rust formation. Which of the four treatment methods had been most successful in halting the effects of the organism? He had conducted the tests on the samples; but the samples were coded. The coding key was in Canberra at the NARRC. They had to match up the test results with the coding to determine which treatment had been most successful. It was part of the blind control method used to assure minimal research bias as a threat to reliability of the results. The encouraging fact was that two of the control procedures had produced very high results. A third procedure had produced modest results. It appeared the fourth procedure did not work. Applying research results to commercial agriculture, it would be devastating to use the wrong procedure.

After this post test was complete, the results could be compared soon with actual field harvest records. Then the results would have meaning for future treatment if the problem were to arise again. Because of careful controls, the results should be generalizable to all of the major wheat growing regions of Australia. That meant that as soon as problems began to appear next spring in either the Darling Downs of western Queensland or in the eastern wheat regions of Western Australia, most of the crop could be salvaged by early treatment with either of the two treatments which had worked with positive results.

Ngarrie's concern was that his analysis and the actual sample bottles might have gone astray. He still had copies of the results by coded number; but, proper procedure called for using the coding numbers as they actually appeared on the bottles. This could create a small glitch in the research procedure and raise some question about the reliability of the research.

Ngarrie had two reasons to be concerned. First, there was substantial federal research money tied to the project. Dr. Nigel Harrington did not look kindly on anything which might raise doubts about research completed in projects under his ultimate direction. Harrington got lots of research dollars because of the impeccable record of his research. Not one hint of error. This would be a hint of an error. The second problem was Ngarrie's own future. As a doctoral student of Harrington's he was expected to function at Dr. Harrington's standards of research. If not, he would not receive a good recommendation from Harrington.

Ngarrie knew he had a serious problem. He immediately sent off an E-mail to the NARRC asking for confirmation that his shipment had been received. Within two minutes his terminal 'pinged' signaling him that he had incoming E-mail. He quickly clicked on New Mail and brought up the item. The reply was a simple terse Reply to his message. The screen seemed to glare at him "NOT RECEIVED."

Ngarrie momentarily froze. His mind went to work. He could not hide this problem. The last thing to do was try to hide bad news from Dr. Harrington. Ngarrie quickly printed out a

copy of the E-mail and headed for Harrington's office just down
the hall.

# WESTERN KANSAS

Delbert Kettering had completed a drive around 800 of his 1200 acres of wheat. He was stunned. The signs of rust infestation were appearing in over half the fields. It was worst in the western fields and less as he moved to the eastern fields. The implication was clear. the infestation had arrived from counties to the west and was moving in an easterly direction. Westerly winds were obviously a factor in spreading the cause of the infestation.

Delbert stopped alongside one of his fields before heading home. As he looked across the fields his thoughts were reviewing what he had seen and what it might mean to him, to his family, and to his neighbors.

The damage in the most westerly fields was extensive and nearly irreversible. Even if a solution could be found and applied immediately, the reduction in crop production would be substantial in those fields. There was little time before damage to adjoining easterly fields would have an effect on production. Del was very concerned. He knew that research at the University of Kansas labs might take days or even weeks to find a cure. Applying a cure, when one was found, could take more days or even weeks.

Driving into the homestead, Delbert surveyed his home, the barns, his expensive equipment. Like all large wheat farmers, he operated on narrow margins. After planting seed, applying fertilizer and pesticide, and considering equipment operating costs; he then had to pay loan costs. No one farmed without a bank or government loan agency as a silent partner in their operation. There was hired help to pay during harvesting, if there was going to be a harvest. Crop failure could be devastating. Del was fortunate that he owned most of the land outright. He could probably servive one year of crop failure. Most other wheat farmers could not. Farmers west of Del were probably almost ruined already. Those to the east were definitely in danger if the rust infestation spread as it seemed to be spreading.

Del turned the pickup motor off and stepped out of the cab. He was met by Sam the collie. Sam bounded up and licked Del's face as a greeting. This brought the first smile of the day to Del's face. Del took the moments to return Sam's affection by giving him a good rub down of his head and neck.

Rachael met Del at the door with a glass of wine. His neighbors drank beer or lemonade depending on their beliefs in temperance. Del liked everything in moderation. But, he hated beer. He had learned to enjoy a glass of wine in the afternoon or a glass of sherry before bedtime. Not many Kansas wheat farmers drank wine and were married to a highly educated woman who could surf the internet as easily as she could bake the best cherry pie in the county. As Rachael handed Del the glass of wine she looked into his eyes and knew that he was troubled.

"What did you find in the fields? Is it getting worse?"

"The rust is spreading rapidly. The wind seems to carry spores or virus or something. Two fields on the western edge of our operation are severely damaged. If we don't find something soon the plants can't come back. And, its spreading."

Rachael knew the implication of what Del was saying. She didn't need to see the concern in his eyes or hear the worry in his voice. But, it was there. She knew. He knew that she knew. Plant stems would be weakened by the rust. Then, winds would topple them over. Once the stem broke there was little hope of saving the plants. Nutrients could not make it up the plant stem to the leaves where photosynthesis normally took place. Multiply that by millions of plants and it meant crop failure.

"Have you heard anything from Lawrence?" asked Del.

"Nothing yet," Rachael replied. "I was on the 'croppers discussion' group on the internet about an hour ago. 'Charlie' over by the Colorado line has lost eighty percent of his crop. It happened in less than ten days."

'Charlie' was not the real name. Few people on computer 'discussion groups' actually used their own name. Rachael signed on to the 'group' by the name of 'Rake.' Ra for Rachael and ke for Kettering. No one in the 'group' knew that. In fact, some might not have accepted her in the 'group' if they knew Rake was a female. All she shared was that Rake hailed from western Kansas.

'Roscoe' up by Manhatten found his first sign of rust yesterday," continued Rachael. Del had a hunch he knew who 'Roscoe' was. He guessed it was probably Robert Scobein who was a large wheat farmer near Manhatten.

"When you are on with the group later today try to suggest that 'Roscoe' get in touch with the research lab at KU. He is going to have the rust spread rapidly. If we can get him in touch with a central research center maybe something can be discovered which will help all of us. There has to be a solution. At least some way to manage the problem."

Del thought about all that he and his ancestors had been through in Kansas trying to grow wheat. The wheat was hybrid of course; but it was hybrid developed from the root stock of Red Turkish wheat. The root stock had been crossed with several varieties to control for effects of weather, insects, and bacteria. The hybrid Red Turkish had served western Kansas wheat farmers well. They had survived the drought of the 1930's Dust Bowl and the various hoards of insects in the 1950's. Each change in the hybrid had improved its performance. Yet, each improvement had moved the gene pool of the seed grain a bit further from the influence of the strength of the root stock Red Turkish. Del knew genetics. He pondered whether something in the seed had made it vulnerable to some sort of bacteria.

Most of the western Kansas wheat farmers used the same type of hybrid sold under different labels. Why not? Many of them were descendants of Ukranian Germans who migrated to Kansas in the 1880's. The hardy immigrants of the 1880's had fled the agricultural regions of the Ukraine to escape persecution of Germans which had occurred in Tsarist Russian control of the

Ukranian lands. The immigrants fled with their families and a few seeds of their favorite sturdy Red Turkish grain which had been the staple for decades. Some fled to Australia. A handful fled to the west central regions of Canada. Most fled to the United States and settled in western Kansas.

Del's family, the Ketterings, were descendants of the Ukranian Germans who came to western Kansas. His great grandfather acquired 160 acres in 1883. His grandfather acquired 800 acres of failed land in the 1930's. Del's father had added more land, consolidated their operations, and modernized everything. Del graduated from the University of Kansas majoring in Agriculture and biology. He and Rachael, with her business and computer skills, were still modernizing the operation. They were a generation ahead of the other descendants of Ukranian Germans in western Kansas. Del knew that and assumed a kind of leadership role. In that leadership role he had forged a link between agriculture and University research which was uncommon anywhere else in the United States and Canada. He felt more comfortable in this kind of leadership role than he would have in entering politics.

"Del," called Rachael, "there's a phone call for you. Can you get it on the other line? I'm downloading some new commodity report data from Washington."

"Got it here," Del replied.

"Hello."

"Del Kettering? This is Martin White of the Kansas City Star."

"Yes. What can I do for you."

"I am a writer with the Star. I just picked up information about some problems with the wheat crop in western Kansas. KU said you might be able to fill me in. We might want to do a story."

"I don't know how much help I can be. Yes, there seems to be a problem developing with the crop."

"What kind of problem?" asked Martin.

"It seems to be an early form of rust which might devastate the crop before it establishes strong supporting stems. That could mean a complete crop failure."

"Bad news for farmers, right?"

"Definitely. And for consumers. Wheat is a staple. Short supply means high food prices."

"Listen Mr. Kettering, could I drive out this evening and interview you? Perhaps we might get some pictures tonight or tomorrow?"

"Sure. I'll be here this evening."

Del, like most western Kansas farmers, was a bit hesitant to talk too much to media types. But he realized this was a serious problem. Perhaps any exposure of the problem might elicit an idea for a solution. Del was cautious with the media people, but he was modern enough to realize today's farmer could not survive without communicating with the world and the world's potential markets.

# SYDNEY

Jeff Spencer was sitting in his hotel room overlooking beautiful Hyde Park in downtown Sydney, Australia. He was pondering his next move in pursuing background for his story on Australian agriculture. He had heard about an interesting year the farmers had in the Darling Downs west of Brisbane. He thought there might be enough human interest in how farmers 'downunder' struggle and survive. He had a contact with an Australian agricultural journal based in Brisbane. His contact there had suggested he might find good information by contacting agricultural experts in Toowoomba, a moderately sized agricultural town on the eastern edge of the Darling Downs region.

Most people outside of Australia knew little about Australian agriculture and practically nothing about the Darling Downs, which is in fact one of the worlds most productive farming regions.

Jeff thought of all kinds of interesting aspects of a feature story he could develop. Maybe he could sell the story in media markets in the United States and Canada.

After obtaining the phone number of Harry Winsome, his contact in Toowoomba, Jeff dialed. Harry Winsome was Public Affairs Director with the Queensland Agricultural Extension office in Toowoomba. Jeff dialed direct and waited through three sets of double rings. Jeff found it hard to adjust to the Australian Telecom double rings. Each ring was really two short rings. It was really stranger than driving on the opposite side of the road. After four double rings there was a reply.

"QAE. Winsome speaking. How may I help you?"

Jeff hesitated a moment, puzzled. "QAE?," he said as a question.

"Queensland Agricultural Extension. Harry Winsome here. May I help you."

"Oh, sorry I was so slow. This is Jeff Spencer calling from Sydney. I am a free lance reporter from the United States. I was given your name and number by a farm reporter colleague of mine in Brisbane."

"Roit."

"I heard that some of the farmers in your region have had some problems with their crops this past year. I understand there was a near failure of the crops."

"Roit. Most of the wheat farmers had a tough go early on and almost lost their crop. Would have been tough for them and for Australia."

"How so," asked Jeff.

"Wheat is an important crop for the consumer market here. Bread. Cereal. Pizza. Meat Pies. And then even some feed grains. Aussies eat pretty much the same things you Americans do. Crop failure would be serious."

"How so?"

"Could have meant having to buy wheat on the international market. Australia hasn't done that for over sixty years. In fact wheat is one of our major export crops. We compete in some of the same world markets as you Yanks and your cousins the Canadians. Luckily we have opposite seasons."

"What happened," asked Jeff.

"Early on in the spring the wheat developed a strange rust problem. Spread like wildfire going through the eucalypt."

"The what?"

"The eucalyptus trees. When we have serious fires out of control they rush through our native eucalyptus trees. Same thing was happening to the rust spreading through the wheat."

"What happened to the farmers?"

"Wonderful story. Through some early detection by the Queensland Agriculture Extension blokes and some hot shot researcher down your way at Maquarie University and the national folks in Canberra they found the cause in time to correct the problem and save seventy percent of the crop. They solved it although they are still verifying tests to determine the best solution."

"Sounds exciting. I would like to do a story. If I come up can you put me in touch with some farmers and officials who could shed some light?" asked Jeff.

"No worries mate. Come on up and I'll take me a holiday so I can take you to see some farmers and introduce you to some folks here in the office. Before you come you should read a report we have prepared for Canberra describing what happened. It's pretty technical but accurate. Even better yet, get yourself across the harbor out to Maquarie University out in Ryde. They did the real scientific detective work and cracked the case."

"Who would I see," asked Jeff as he scribbled information.

"Officially, you need to talk to Dr. Nigel Harrington. He's Director down there. Better yet talk to Ngarrie Bhojammie. He is a hot shot researcher in the lab who actually cracked the case. Can you imagine that, an abo who is an expert on crops?"

"I wasn't aware," replied Jeff.

"Even better yet, start with Karen Stone. She's secretary in the lab. She'll smooth the contacts for you with Harrington and N.B."

"N.B.?" asked Jeff.

"Ngarrie. He prefers being less formal. Five minutes after you meet him he will be N.B. Trust me."

"Thanks for your help. I will be looking for the report. Then I would like to come up. Will you mail the report.?"

"How about if I fax it to you. Then you can come up later this week. There are some horse races later this week out west of Toowoomba. That's when I would like for you to need my services to take you around the country. Friday this week would be a good day. Races that day. Isn't that the day you will need my services?"

"Are you sure this is convenient," asked Jeff.

"No worries, mate. This is my job. I like to do my job well. And in this case I can do it best on Friday. See you later this week."

Jeff smiled as he hung up the telephone. He was pleased the report would be faxed to his hotel. He could make the arrangement to go out to Maquarie. He chuckled at the speed with which Harry Winsome facilitated his contacts. He knew that Australians loved to go to the horse races. He also knew they often jumped at the chance to get away from work. Showing an American journalist around was plenty of excuse.

Jeff left the room headed for the New South Wales State Library. He had some reading to do on Australian Agriculture. He could walk the six blocks to the library quickly. If he took a slight detour, he could grab an Aussie pie for lunch at a street stand and stroll down to the Botanic Garden, have lunch and then on to the Library. That would be a bit out of the way; but, he felt 'why not?'

# SYDNEY

About the time Jeff was heading for the New South Wales State Library, Aaron was waiting for Jennifer Cross, the Sydney Herald intern, to meet her across George Street at a coffee shop in the Strand. Jennifer had been snooping for her to discover what the police knew about the murder at the Opera House. Aaron was intrigued by the event. She was always intrigued by strange or puzzling events. Jennifer was an eager intern assigned to Aaron. She could get away with some basic investigation, which was really snooping, where Aaron could not. Jennifer could be excused for making a novice 'mistake.' Aaron could not.

Aaron thought about how she let herself be pulled into high profile cases. Last year it was a murder of a staff member at the Indonesian consulate which captured her interest. The murder happened in a crowd at the Cricket grounds. As it turned out it was a small event in a large corporate spying operation. The police didn't want her involved then either. She and Jeff stumbled onto the clues hidden in a warehouse out in Parrammata. The size of the operation and the scope of government officials in both countries involved with private companies was staggering. She recalled how the obscure murder exploded into a rather testy international issue. She and Jeff turned up the clues, virtually solved the case and turned it over to the police. Finally, the police appreciated what she and Jeff had done, but they really didn't like 'civilians' interfering. Especially when it showed them up. The only salvation was that when her staff person at the Herald got the scoop, and wrote the story, he gave a lot of good press to the police. They seemed to be the heroes. Only she, Jeff, the reporter, and of course the police, knew differently.

She was just beginning to recall how she and Jeff had similar experiences two years ago with an abduction in the Asian community. She was recalling how that escapade had gone when she spied Jennifer almost running up the steps of the Strand to where they were meeting for coffee.

"Aaron, I'm sorry to be running late," apologized Jennifer Cross. She slid into the chair across from Aaron and dropped her briefcase.

"No worries. Let me get you something. Tea? Coffee? Stronger?"

"A strong coffee, replied Jennifer." Jennifer was anxious to show that she could succeed at whatever task Aaron gave her.

"Any success?" asked Aaron.

"Some. I found out what the police know." Jennifer was pulling out her lap top computer to check her notes which she carried on a floppy disk.

Aaron smiled realizing that this act signaled the generational difference. Aaron learned her journalism with a notebook. Her high tech was a tape recorder for interviews. Today, young eager interns like Jennifer carried a small computer. They put everything on floppy disks. The tape recording was done by a miniature recorder carried in her small purse and activated by turning the knob which looked like the latch cover on the side of the purse.

"The police know the subject was a loner. He was carrying a computer disk in his suitcoat pocket. They are still trying to decipher what is on it, but they seem to be treating the disk as incidental. He had been a regular at the Opera House. Bought a season ticket the first day they went on sale."

"Those were not cheap seats," commented Jennifer. Was he a big spender?"

"Doesn't seem that he was. Owned his small home out near Bondi. Small two bedroom bungalow. No large accounts at any known banks. No immediately known local relatives. He had another spending habit."

"Oh, what's that?" asked Jennifer.

"Liked the races."

"What Australian doesn't. We all bet. Betting on the horses is as common as eating vegemite."

"No, he was a regular. Every week. But he only bet small amounts. Won some. Lost some. No indication he had big debts."

"Somebody was after him for some reason. What did he do on his job? Wasn't he some kind of courier?"

"Yes, he worked for a North Sydney Courier company. Police have interviewed his boss at his company and found nothing."

"Nothing," repeated Jennifer. "I don't believe it."

"That's what the police found."

"Are you sure?"

"Yes, I'm sure," replied Jennifer.

"How can you be so sure?"

"I'd rather not say?"

Jennifer smiled. "I won't pressure you on your source, but just explain how you can be so sure the police found nothing at that North Sydney Courier company."

Aaron hesitated. "I have a friend who is doing an internship in communications at the police station. I don't want to get him into any trouble, but I believe him when he assures me they found nothing."

"OK. I'll buy that. Now, there is something there. The fact that the police didn't find anything out intrigues me. You don't happen to know anyone over there at the courier company do you?"

"Afraid not. In fact I'm not very good yet at investigative reporting into the corporate world."

Aaron realized the intern had done well. She had gone as far as she could go. She would have to get into the corporate world herself. She was good at that. Jeff knew how to help.

"Great work, Jennifer. Keep a close ear to what you can find through the police. I'll take care of the corporate angle."

Jennifer looked saddened.

"I believe you have done good work. You're still learning. I appreciate what you have been able to do. Check with me here tomorrow, same time. O.K.?"

"O.K."

Jennifer left down the same stair. Aaron was about to leave when she saw Jeff coming into the Strand. She would hold the table and have another coffee with him.

"Well, you look pleased. What's happening?" asked Aaron.

Jeff slid into the seat Jennifer had recently vacated. He smiled at Aaron. "I'm always pleased when I find the most beautiful person in Sydney."

Aaron leaned forward setting her coffee down slowly. "Thanks for the compliment, but I really doubt that I turn you on in the middle of the morning in the Strand Mall."

"Never know the power of beauty," replied Jeff. "However, in addition to the power of your beauty I have had some good luck with my research. That always makes me happy. When I'm happy I appreciate beauty more than ever."

"What have you found?"

"There is possibly a great human interest story which has unfolded in Queensland. There has been this threat to the wheat crop which stumped farmers, botanists, and agronomists. My contact in Brisbane reports that some quick research by some chaps at Macquarie University solved the problem, came up with a solution, and virtually saved the wheat farmers. It has a great human interest angle. Farmers threatened. Science intervenes. Science saves farmers."

"And saves Australian consumers," added Aaron. "Agriculture is just as important in the Aussie society as it is for you Yanks."

"Great. That makes and even greater universal appeal to the story. How's the case coming? I assume you are pursuing that murder at the Opera House."

Jeff caught the eye of a waiter and nodded for another coffee for himself and Aaron.

"Yes," replied Aaron. "It seems just like another murder case, but how many happen at the Opera House in Sydney?"

"Definitely not your usual," added Jeff.

"I guess I am intrigued because it is so unusual. It's also unusual because the victim seemed like the last person one might want to murder. What we are finding bears that out. He was a simple person. Worked as a courier for a communication company located in North Sydney. Basically, he transported things. Documents. Objects. Books."

"Isn't that a bit antiquated today," asked Jeff. "I thought in this electronic age everything got transmitted by some electronic means."

"Basically, most things do. But, there are still some things which have to be carried by a human."

"Like what?" asked Jeff.

"Like research objects you want someone else to analyze for confirming analysis. Like some highly secret data files. Sending them electronically always has a risk that someone will steal information. So, there are still times when a human needs to physically transport an object. It is usually transferred by a highly protected means; like, in an armored vehicle."

"But, this guy wasn't in an armored vehicle," commented Jeff.

"Right. That's one of the reasons this case intrigues me. He was a simple person who apparently didn't carry his work in a highly visible fashion. It looks like he traveled very publicly using mass transportation. Car. Bus. Train. Plane. Whatever. The point is he traveled in a fashion which did not attract attention. Yet, the company he worked for is noted for transporting and or communicating things, including information, which is often highly secret in nature."

Jeff nodded. "I see what you mean about intriguing. The fact he was so common and used such common means could likely mask the significance of the role he was playing. Unless someone found out."

"Right. So, I have an intern who has been reasonably successful finding out for me what the police know. What she can not do is crack the corporate barrier. That is where I come in. I am going to North Sydney this afternoon and see what I can

George E. Tuttle

find out from TRANSCOM, Inc. That is the company which employed Stanley Hutch. Want to come with me?"

"Sure. Someone will need to keep you out of deep trouble again. Remember the last two escapades."

"Yes. I got what the police couldn't in each case, but both times I needed your help. Let's take the tube over to North Sydney."

"Not the harbor ferry? It is always such a nice scenic ride. The tube just goes under the harbor. Nothing to see."

"The tube is quicker. Maybe we can take the ferry back."

Just as they were beginning to arise, they were approached by Lieutenant Ed Wilson of the Sydney Police Department.

"Just who I wanted to see," he said approaching their table."

"Lieutenant, how did you know where to find me," asked Aaron with a cautious tone to her voice.

"Let's just say I know where to find you when I want to," replied Wilson. "I want to talk with you quietly off the record about the Hutch case."

"Of course, Lieutenant," replied Aaron with a smile to Wilson and an unobtrusive wink to Jeff. "I am not certain how I can help."

"Come on, Miss Worthington. I know you are involved in this case just as you were with a case last year and the year before. I think we might be able to help each other. We want to solve a case. You want to solve a case. It happens to be the same case."

"How can I be of any help? It's the police that have all of the legal powers to investigate."

"Legal is the operative word, Miss Worthington. You have some opportunities we do not have."

"You know I can't reveal sources, Lieutenant."

"Of course not. We wouldn't want that at all," replied Wilson.

Jeff smiled. He knew that Aaron and Wilson were in a sparing match. He thought this was indeed revealing. The last two times the police were angered with Aaron's involvement.

70

They didn't like civilians interfering with a case. They had even threatened her with arrest. She had ignored their warnings and played a major role in cracking both cases. She got information the police could not get. It was interesting to note that the Lieutenant in his request for Aaron's help was arguing precisely from that premise. Now, instead of seeing her as a hindrance they saw her as a resource. The police in Sydney were not stupid.

"I'm wondering Lieutenant," Aaron said in a careful tone, "what motivation there might be for me to work so closely with the police?"

"Several reasons. Let me begin with civic duty. We all live in this fair city and every citizen needs to help keep it a safe place. As you well know, the police can not do that alone."

"And what else, Lieutenant?"

"Let me skip all the in-between reasons and get to the most basic practical reason. Your own personal gratification with solving interesting puzzles. You help us, we can help you."

"I am not certain how I can see you helping me."

Wilson smiled as he replied softly. "How do you think your lovely intern has been able to obtain information which we have. She has been working on one of our handsome young officers. She thinks he is her secret inside source. And he is. We find that a potentially useful channel of communication. Now I would like to expand the channel a bit more directly between you and I."

Aaron showed little surprise, but Jeff knew she had been stunned by Wilson's offer. Obviously Wilson not only recognized how helpful she could be; but, also knew how to persuade her to participate.

"Lieutenant," replied Aaron cautiously, "let me be certain the ground rules are straight. You provide me with your leads and information through 'leaks' in your department and I offer you any helpful information I find. But, no sources. Is that clear?"

"Agreed."

"How do I get information to you?"

71

Lieutenant Wilson smiled and replied quietly. "I assume Jeff here is more than just a casual American journalist. I suggest that you have him make a call to me to report a suspicious incident which occurred at a certain time. I will know that is a signal to meet with you or Jeff or both of you right here at that time during the next twelve hours."

"Lieutenant," protest Jeff, "upon what basis do you conclude something about the nature of the relationship between Aaron and myself?"

"Please, Mr. Spencer. Don't make me reveal just how much we do know."

"Fine," replied Aaron. "You are correct. Jeff is involved and is completely trustworthy. You will help, won't you Jeff."

"Sure," replied Jeff.

Wilson arose. As he was leaving, he nodded and said, "ta."

"Can you believe that. He has known all along what I was trying to do." Aaron was clearly surprised and a bit angry.

They exited the Strand and crossed the street to catch the tube at Wynyard Station. From there it was quickly up and across the Sydney Bridge, through the Molson Point Station, and then to North Sydney. The entire trip from the time they left the second floor of the Strand Cafe had taken exactly fifteen minutes. Aaron checked her miniature computerized city directory and located the address for the TRANSCOM company. It was a short three block walk.

"What are we after," asked Jeff?

"We are looking for whatever we can find out about the usual or occasional work of our poor dead courier, Stanley Hutch. Which clients he carried for. Any unusual habits he had. Any work companions he socialized with. Something may turn up."

They strolled the three blocks quickly. The building in front of them carried the address listed in Aaron's Directory. The building was nondescript. It was a small, narrow two story building in an area of offices and small business buildings. There was a warning sign on the front entrance intended to deter would be burglars. The brick building could house any kind of small business. As they stepped through the front entry way, Jeff was aware that a faint buzzing sound interrupted the soft elevator music playing through the hidden speakers. As they entered they had broken a hidden laser beam  which announced their presence.

They opened an inside door and stepped into a small softly lighted room. A secretary look up from her plain desk, the only furniture in the room. The sign on her desk said she was Desiree Lamoine.

"May I help you?" she asked.

"I am Aaron Worthington from the Sydney Herald. This is my associate Jeff Spencer."

The expression on the receptionist face immediately changed from business helpful to business media wary.

"You had an employee, Stanley Hutch. He was recently killed in the Opera House. I have an interest in the case. Can you tell me about Mr. Hutch?"

"I believe you will need to talk with our manager. He isn't in right now. Perhaps I can make an appointment."

Jeff who had been standing near the window commented, "Someone just came in from a car parked in the space reserved for the manager. Perhaps he will see us. It's very important. He probably would rather talk to us now than have us draw some misconceptions."

"Let me check with him." With that the receptionist retreated quickly through the doorway behind her and down the hall to her right.

Aaron smiled at Jeff. "Thanks. You were observant."

" Yes, but not quite what it seemed. I saw two cars parked. I assumed one was hers. The other might be the manager."

Aaron stepped over to the window and looked. "Good bluff."

The receptionist returned to the doorway. "The manager, Mr. LeBalme will see you," she said with a false sweet voice. "This way, please."

As they stepped down the dark hall Jeff noticed the several doors to rooms they passed. Each seemed to be a small room. Perhaps a work room for various labeling or sorting. If so, each was for a small operation. Perhaps each courier had his or her own small work cubicle. So far the building seemed more like an office building than a warehouse for storing or sorting products to be transported.

As the receptionist ushered Aaron and Jeff through the last door they were greeted by a firm voice. "Welcome. Please be seated. I'm Renard LaBalme. How can I help you?"

"I am Aaron Worthington of the Sydney Herald and my associate Jeff Spencer from the United States." After hand shaking was completed, Aaron continued. "We are looking into some of the circumstances surrounding the unfortunate death of one of your couriers, Stanley Hutch."

"We are most saddened by Mr. Hutch's misfortune to be in the wrong place at the wrong time," replied LaBalme.

"Actually I have some problems with the theory of being in the wrong place at the wrong time," interjected Aaron. "Not many murders occur at the Opera House, except on stage in a few operas. Rather, the police records reveal no other instance of such an event. Neither do the records of the Sydney Herald."

A wrinkle was beginning to form on LaBalme's forehead. Jeff noticed the wrinkle and his eye was drawn to a map behind LaBalme with several cities in Australia and Indonesia circled. He made a note to ask about the map.

Aaron was continuing with her explanation bringing a deeper wrinkle to LaBalme's forehead. "The police consider the act murder. I agree. Someone knew his behavior. They knew the score of the concert for that night. They knew where he would be and the opportune time to commit murder by firing a gun in the least noticeable time and place. The only plausible theory is that he was a target. Why?"

"I have no idea," replied LaBalme obviously abandoning the theory of random murder. "Perhaps there was something in Mr. Hutch's private life we do not know about."

"Possibly. But, not likely. The police have found nothing at his home except some bottles he was perhaps transporting as part of his job with TRANSOM."

"Nothing else?" LaBalme asked in a puzzled voice.

"Nothing else," replied Aaron. "What else should there have been?"

"Nothing," replied LaBalme quickly. Too quickly to suit Jeff.

"What about the bottles?" asked Aaron.

"Just a routine transport of objects from a client in the Sydney area to Canberra," replied LaBalme.

"Contents?" asked Jeff.

"No idea," replied LaBalme.

"You have no idea?"

"None. We just contract to pick up and deliver. If we have some doubt about the legality we have the sender sign an assumption of legal responsibility." LaBalme was sounding calmer but still had one deep wrinkle on his forehead. Something was worrying him.

"Was he transporting anything else?" asked Jeff.

"No," replied LaBalme with another deep wrinkle appearing on his forehead again.

Aaron looked directly at LaBalme. She spoke slowly and with a firmer voice. "Mr. LaBalme, my research indicates that you have had several indictments for obstruction of justice in Queensland. What are you holding out?"

Jeff had moved such that he could see the papers on the corner of LaBalme's desk. He noted a list with items checked off. During the exchange between Aaron and LaBalme he noticed that everything was checked off except two items. He was straining to read the item and thought he could discern the word 'bottle' and 'disk.' As Aaron and LaBalme were frozen in a locked stare he asked casually, "What about the disk?"

LaBalme reacted like he had been shot. His eyes flew to his desk. His hand started to move toward the corner of his desk. Jeff grabbed the list, stepped back around Aaron to the window, glanced quickly at the list. If Aaron had not been there, LaBalme might have leaped over the desk to retrieve the list. He froze midway around the desk as Aaron stepped to her left injecting herself in the new path between LaBalme and Jeff.

Jeff read from the list, "Bengotti disk. What is that Mr. LaBalme?"

"That is private. Return that now, Mr. Spencer." All hint of friendliness was gone from LaBalme's voice.

Jeff stepped around Aaron and handed the list to LaBalme. "It's a clients list, isn't it? Every name is checked off except Bengottis."

"Tell us about the client Mr. LaBalme," ordered Aaron. "I will find out eventually. However, if you make me waste time investigating I will let the police know you are obstructing justice by hiding a list of important evidence regarding a serious crime. Tell me now and I will let you call the police and volunteer that you just discovered something which might be of interest to them."

There were moments of silence. LaBalme was clearly thinking, weighing his options. Slowly, carefully, he began to speak. "Bengottis refers to Bengotti Imports near here in St. Leonards. We have a contract to transport computer disks by hand for them overnight to various locations. I assume it is to their Australian outlets. Sometimes Hutch is the courier who transports the disk, along with other transports. He was supposed to be carrying a disk from Bengottis to Canberra. It isn't here in his workspace. We assume he had it with him. This is very confidential. Please don't run this information in the Herald. Our business depends upon our maintaining client confidentiality. Please."

Jeff handed over the list to LaBalme. As he did so he asked, "What is the map on the other corner of your desk?"

LaBalme turned and all three looked at a map lying on his desk with lots of circles. "That is a map of our TRANSCOM locations in Australia and Indonesia."

Jeff slowly walked to the map on the corner of the desk. LaBalme began to intercede and stopped. Jeff picked up the map and asked "are these locations all of your business sites?"

"Yes."

"I see there are circles in two different colors—black and red."

"The black ones are our present locations. The red circles are new planned locations."

"There are three red circles. Two of them surround cities. The third has no city inside the circle. What is that?"

"That is an area of future growth. If a city ever goes in we will locate there. Nothing planned for now."

"So, it's likely jungle now?"

"I assume so."

"We need this list and this map," interjected Aaron.

"I can't let those out of this room."

"Mr. LaBalme, let me remind you that you will be calling the police soon to report you 'just discovered some evidence.' I would hate to report that you have been withholding evidence. Remember that is obstruction, a criminal offense in New South Wales."

"I'll make you a copy to take if you promise not to publish either. Publicity would destroy our business."

"Make me a copy. I will agree not to publish them unless I obtain the information from another source."

# RYDE

Aaron and Jeff left the TRANSCOM building and quickly headed for the tube station. They had agreed to split up and each one follow a different lead.

"Jeff, you take the disk lead. Lieutenant Wilson was holding out on us. He has the disk. Go to Bengottis and find out what was on that disk. Maybe they have a backup. Something on there might provide a lead to explain why Hutch was killed. Once we know that, then we will soon know who. I'm taking the bus out to Macquarie University to follow up on the bottle lead."

There was a quick kiss, a prolonged holding hands, eyes met and Aaron finally spoke, "Concert tonight at the Opera House."

"Let's meet for dinner at the Bennelong Restaurant," replied Jeff.

"At five sharp. I have to run. My bus is pulling in now." Aaron broke and dashed down the steps to the bus stop as the 445 bus was arriving from downtown Sydney headed out to North Ryde where the university was located.

As the bus rambled through the streets on its way to North Ryde Aaron had time to think through what was happening. Her thoughts turned to questions. Why was Macquarie University sending bottles with a courier company? What was in those bottles? Where were they being taken to Canberra? Could the answers to any of these questions suggest some reason why Hutch's life had been in danger?

She noticed that the neighborhood she was traveling through now was becoming more upscale. Homes were all single family and newer. Businesses were more neighborhood businesses. Grocery stores, liquor stores, dental offices, chemist shops, meat markets. All grouped in one block to service a neighborhood. All newer brick, air conditioned buildings. Sydney suburbs were evolving much like the urban areas she had seen so often in the United States. Not like the European model. There was more metro planning here. More orderly. People griped about collective social political organization but they hated the opposite.

Now her bus was approaching a new large urban mall. It was the Macquarie Mall named after the large growing university three blocks down the street. This bus terminated its run at the mall. She would walk the three remaining blocks. This was the outer edge of the northwest urban area. From here one had to transfer to busses which ran routes to the far flung still developing areas beyond the university.

All Aaron had to go on was the name of the agency at Macquarie which contracted with the courier company, TRANSCOM. It was the Science Research Center Division. She would have to start there and locate where the bottles came from and who dealt with them.

She walked up the sidewalk toward what she knew was the administrative building. Inside she located the university information office.

"May I help you," asked a pleasant receptionist working at the information desk.

"Yes, I'm looking for the Science Research Division."

"You'll find that two buildings straight away to your left after you leave the building."

"Thank you. I appreciate your help."

"No worries ma'am," replied the young receptionist.

Aaron proceed out of the administration building and turned left. Two buildings on she turned left into an ordinary looking brick building. Hidden behind overgrown bushes was the name, "Science Research."

As she entered the building, Aaron remembered she had done a story over ten years ago about highly secretive plant pathology work being done here under contract to the Australian Army. Something about nerve gas anti toxins extracted from unique rain forest plants. It had been a good story, but some of the best had been withdrawn by her superiors at the Sydney Herald. When she protested she was just informed that the Defense Ministry in Canberra had made a special request that some of the results from joint work with the American military not be included. She remembered that she really fumed at the time. Later she learned there had been a "quid pro quo." She and a photographer had been given exclusive coverage opportunity for joint Australian and American military naval exercises off the coast of the York peninsula. She had decided that she had been paid off. But the Herald and the government in Canberra had a "respectful relationship."

Now Aaron was wondering once again what was going on in this old laboratory. As she entered the main door she found a directory on the right wall. The Science Research Division was listed in room 201. She began her search for 201. The area around the entrance seemed dingy with paper lying in the corners. As she went up the stairway looking for the 200 level rooms she noticed that everything suddenly appeared neater and cleaner. Upon reaching the second level and entering two tightly fitting doors the hall was as antiseptically clean as any hospital. Clearly the first floor was the teaching floor and the second floor was the research floor.

She found room 201 immediately on her right. Upon entering she was greeted by another receptionist. This receptionist was a student type.

"May I help you?" asked the young male student receptionist.

"Yes, I'm looking for the director," replied Aaron.

"That would be Dr. Nigel Harrington."

"I am Aaron Worthington from the Sydney Herald. I need to talk with Dr. Harrington."

"Dr. Harrington isn't in his office at this moment. Could I make an appointment?" asked the student receptionist.

"It is rather urgent that I speak with him as soon as possible. It involves an investigation which is related to a police investigation of a murder." Aaron was walking a thin line. She did not want to be liable for a charge of impersonating a police officer. But, it was true her own investigation was related to the police work and she had tacit approval from Lieutenant Wilson to relate her work to his. She had walked this thin line before.

The student hesitated, clearly a bit uneasy about what to do. Slowly, he replied, "Dr. Harrington is in the building, but truly he is not in his office here."

"Please, pleaded Aaron, "I understand your reluctance to disturb whatever he might be doing, but this really is urgent."

"Well, Dr. Harrington is also Director of the Agronomy Research Lab which is part of the Science Research Division. He is actually in the Agronomy Lab this afternoon. I guess it might be all right for you to talk with him."

"Thank you. Can you direct me to the lab?"

"The lab is a bit difficult to locate. Let me take you down."

They exited the reception room and wound their way through several winding hallways. Some rooms had numbers and some did not. Aaron assumed there was some degree of secrecy regarding some parts of the building. However, there was no visible security which one might expect where military sponsored research might have been or still is being conducted. Soon they arrived at an unmarked room and entered another room which was equipped like an office. There was a secretary working. She looked up as Aaron and the male receptionist entered the room. They exchanged a look and a nod passing on through a door into what was clearly a laboratory.

"Dr. Harrington, I hate to disturb you, but this lady is Aaron Worthington of the Sydney Herald. She has expressed a need to speak to you immediately regarding a police investigation."

"Pleased to meet you, Miss Worthington. Thank you Craig." The male receptionist exited the room.

"How can I be of assistance, Miss Worthington?" asked Harrington.

"You may have heard there was murder at the Opera House."

"Yes, I have. Dreadful happening. We don't have too many. And in the beautiful opera house no less."

"The police are following as many leads as they can. I am trying to help by following some information the police are, shall we say, not able to follow easily."

"Anything I can do to help, I certainly will; but, I fail to see what I can add."

"I have been able to determine that there were some bottles in the possession of the deceased. Further, I was able to determine that those bottles were in the possession of the deceased because he was a courier for a company called TRANSCOM located in North Sydney." Aaron paused as she noticed that Harrington was nodding. "Are you familiar with TRANSCOM?" she asked.

"Yes, I am," replied Harrington. "How do they fit in with your inquiry?"

"According to the people at TRANSCOM the bottles were being carried under assignment to your lab here at Macquarie."

"Yes, we routinely use that service to provide relatively rapid transport of actual objects we have analyzed or that we are returning to some other agency or person. Usually we complete a contracted analysis and report our results by secured electronic means. In some cases there are reasons to retain the actual samples. If we retain them here we store them and there would be no transport needed. If we are working on a project for someone connected with a governmental project, we often transport the actual samples to Canberra for storage there."

"Was there anything about the project or the samples which might cause someone to want to kill a courier?" asked Aaron.

"Nothing I can think of," replied Harrington. The project was a simple analysis of plant residue material from Queensland."

"It wasn't some kind of classified governmental work?"

"If it was, I couldn't discuss that; but, this was a project for the Ministry of Agriculture to identify the pathological structure of some plant material. The data analysis was made and the results sent electronically to Queensland and to Canberra. We assumed Canberra wanted to keep the actual samples. That is the only reason we contracted with TRANSCOM. Sorry I can't be of much help to you. There just isn't anything there that might be the motivation for murder."

"You certain there wasn't anything found in the analysis which someone might want or might want to deny to others?"

"Nothing. Absolutely nothing. A plant cell tissue enzyme was identified. Several people already know about that. It is a matter of public record. Certainly nothing to kill someone over."

"Thank you, Dr. Harrington. I appreciate your time." Aaron turned toward the door to leave. "Please contact me if you become aware of anything else. You can reach me at the Herald."

"If I come across anything which might be useful, I will. Good luck."

Aaron departed from the building much disappointed. She had hoped there might be some lead here as to why anyone might want to murder that poor nice fellow. She walked slowly toward the train station hoping that Jeff was having more success as he followed up the lead on the disk.

# KANSAS CITY

Martin White had just ordered two Napa white wines and began to relax back into his favorite bench in the secluded nook of Henri's Bar. Henri was a rare Frenchman. He tolerated American wines in his wine bar. In fact Martin suspected that he secretly preferred Napa wines to French wines. But, he wouldn't dare say that.

Just as the two glasses were being delivered, Martin was starring across the street at nothing. He was thinking about the latest developments in the strange wheat story he was pursuing. It seemed there was impending disaster confronting Kansas wheat farmers. He had just returned from the University of Kansas in Lawrence. He had hoped he could file a completed story with the Kansas City Star today. But, his interview with chief investigators at the University of Kansas labs had not been completely fruitful. Seems they had not found the underlying cause. He did discover that they were pursuing both organic and non-organic causes. That meant bugs and chemicals. He knew that was two different worlds for scientists.

"Your wines, sir." The waitress placed both glasses in front of Martin. "You a two fisted drinker?

"No, just waiting for a friend. I know what she will have. You look new here." Martin didn't recognize this waitress. He knew that the regulars would know who he was meeting. He and Cindy Nelson were regulars here. Cindy came in after long tedious sessions in the Kansas City Court. He came when he was having difficulty making a story angle work. They both came whenever they wanted to just talk.

There were all kinds of angles for this story; but, he couldn't make any of them lead anywhere. So far all he had was suspense. That had been the angle of his first story filed today. He routinely filed a copy with the AP wire in addition to his own paper's copy. His paper would be able to run first copy before anyone else ran something off the wire.

"Actually, I'm a student at UMKC. Trying to make it through." The University of Missouri at Kansas City was an up and coming stepchild school in the large Missouri higher education system.

"What are you studying?"

"I'd like to be a journalist. Someday. Working my way through school means more like six or seven years rather than four."

"If journalism is your interest, why not study at the main campus in Columbus? They have an outstanding journalism program."

"That is just it. They have a reputation. They won't admit marginal students. They want bright people in and out on time to go out and continue the reputation for the school. I have to work my way or I can't go. I don't fit their 'preferred profile.'"

"Gotcha. I know what you mean. You may make a better journalist if you have to struggle a bit to make it through. You'll understand more aspects of life. That's where stories are usually rooted. Good luck."

As he was sipping his glass and looking again out the window into nothing, Cindy arrived and slide into the bench with him. His first awareness of her presence was a soft nibble on the ear.

"Hey. Where did you come from? Bus late?"

"No, court ran late. The judge was in a foul mood today."

"What happened? Did you show contempt for the court or something?"

"No, not quite. I lost my cool with the defense attorney. He is a Neanderthal trying to defend a Neanderthal who committed spousal abuse."

"Hey, whoa. Where is this innocent until proven guilty philosophy which is the backbone of our judicial system?"

"This ape is not innocent. You should have seen what this woman's face looked like when he finished."

"What did the defense attorney say to set you off?"

85

"It's not what he said. It was how he and his client were both looking at me during my cross examination of one of his witnesses."

"How they looked at you? How can you take offense at that?"

"They virtually undressed me with their looks. It was horrible."

"So how did you lose your cool?"

"I asked his witness if he had not seen the accused beating his wife in the face like a caveman tossing his cave partner around?"

"No kidding. I rather imagine the judge did not take well to your question. Perhaps the defense attorney objected with that pained look on his face."

"Yes, I blew it. Tomorrow, I will not blow it. I will be cool. Now, let's talk about civilized people. How did your interviews go today? Got your story on the wheat problem?"

"I've got a story filed; but, I'm just as frustrated as you are. For very different reasons, of course."

"What's your problem?" Cindy was glad for a change of subject. She really was interested in whatever problem Martin was having. They often helped solve each other's professional problems.

"No one has a solution. The lab people haven't found the cause of the rust. It doesn't seem to be the same kind of cell and chemical action typical of rust."

"Who's working on this?"

"The very best we have. Some of the top agronomist and plant botanic scientists in the world work at the KU Lab. It's being headed by Dr. Wilson Blaine. "

"How bad is the problem?"

"It's really serious to a lot of Kansas farmers; and thus, to the Kansas economy. Millions of acres are planted in wheat. It seems this blight—rust—whatever you want to call it, started in eastern Colorado in the winter wheat and has spread across into much of western Kansas. It would appear that it must be spread by wind. The prevailing winds are westerly and that is the path of the spread of the rust."

"What are farmers doing? Can't they re-seed or put in some other crop? How about something to stop the rust?"

"Stop the rust if they could. Scientists can't find the cause, so they can't find how to neutralize whatever it is. It's too late to replant either wheat or the only other option, milo. There is a wheat farmer from out in western Kansas brought in a sample for testing. It seems he and his wife are pretty modern farmers."

"How so?"

"It seems she is a whiz on the internet and with modern communications. She had the Governor of Kansas, the Federal Agriculture people, and the scientists at the University of Kansas all alerted to the problem within hours after her husband found the first signs of the rust in their crop. She had the politicians and scientists all scurrying by the time her husband could make the three hour drive from Emden to Lawrence. As soon as he arrived, they began testing. So far no results."

"What kind of tests do they do?"

"Oh some simple analysis of structure to identify the substance through comparisons with know rust strains which they maintain in a data bank. Nothing. That was the quick analysis. Then they began some more detailed analyze which take more time. One of them produces fairly quick results. That is a breakdown of cell structure comparing any abnormalities with a data bank of known abnormalities."

"And did they find abnormalities?"

"Oh, they found abnormalities. But, they didn't match anything in the data bank."

"So, they are looking at a new something or other? Right?"

"Right. Now the longer testing has to systematically look at how various amino acids and acid combinations interact with the sample."

"Won't that take a long time?"

"It might, unless they are lucky. The various samples have to sit for several days before they know the results for sure."

87

"Who was this farmer from Emden," asked Cindy.

"Someone named Kettering," replied Martin. "Delbert Kettering. He's a big wheat spread out in west central Kansas. They live near Emden."

"And, what did you say his wife's name was? The one who is the computer whiz?" asked Cindy.

"Um, let me see," replied Martin as he began checking his notes. he recognized the look of disgust on Cindy's face. "I know, I'm a chauvinist. I knew his name, Delbert; but, I didn't remember her name. No it didn't make as much impression on me," he apologized as he found his notes. "Her name is Rachael, Rachael Kettering."

Cindy's face went from her expression of annoyance with Martin to gradually show a kind of surprise. "What is it?" asked Martin.

"I know her. Martin, I know her. We were sorority sisters in college. She was majoring in business and computer science. I was in political science and then went on to law school."

Martin's face lit up. He sat up, reached for Cindy's arm. smiled, and said: "You know her. Are you certain it is the same person. She would not have been Kettering when you were in school."

"I know; but, she was not a party girl. She was serious about this Kansas wheat country farmer. She always volunteered to serve drinks and the like at sorority functions because she wasn't going with anyone local or on the make for anyone. It has to be the same person. That would be too much of a coincidence."

Martin's face was reflecting his inner excitement. This might be a break. If nothing else it would add another human interest dimension to his story which had already been filed. If he could actually interview real farmers who are trying to cope with impending disaster it would be a great follow up. "Do you think you can get away to drive out to Emden to talk with her," asked Martin. "You could really help me with this contact."

Cindy had to think fast. She really wanted to help Martin. It might be great for their relationship. She had to do some research tomorrow for her case in court later in the week. "Let's go to my office," said Cindy. "I need to do two things. First, we need to see if we can contact the Ketterings. If she is so active on the internet she probably has a listed e-mail address. With a search I may be able to find it. Then we need to contact her and be certain they will be there if we make that four hour drive. Second, I need to give my research assistant some specific directions about getting me a delay in court tomorrow. I still have the unpleasant task in court tomorrow, remember. "

# ST. LEONARDS

Frank Bengotti was reflecting on the fact that it had been over an hour and three pizzas since their computer ace, Harrold Lassiter, had started working to locate who was breaking into their security system. Frank worried a lot about just such a security problem. That is why he convinced brother, Al, they needed to bring Lassiter into the business.

Their ability to make a profit depended upon a complicated purchase and delivery system of exotic tropical plants quickly to all major cities in Australia. Most exotic tropical plants sold in Australia were in fact grown in northern Queensland. In the far north the climate did support nursery growth of such plants, but it was slow and costly.

They had an advantage over competitors because of their secret sources of plants deep in the jungles of Indonesia. The plants flourished in a natural environment. The growth was quick and cheap. Labor was cheap. The supply operation was run very efficiently by younger brother, Renaldo. Renaldo Bengotti had been the only one of three brothers to go to university. He had studied biology at University of New South Wales while he worked at various odd jobs in the greater Sydney area. But he liked to travel. He had taken every opportunity to travel to unusual places on biology field trips. He had become enthralled by the exotic plants throughout the various tropical regions of the world. It was natural behavior for him to join his older brothers in the nursery plant business. In fact it had been Renaldo who suggested the idea of growing plants in a tropical zone like Indonesia to get faster growth. At the same time they could get quick access to different and exotic plants.

The Bengottis had a system in place for delivering quality goods inexpensively for shipment through an unlikely port in Port Douglas. The plants were clean. The plants cleared agricultural customs easily. For all suppliers, and competitors for that matter, knew they were growing the plants in a nursery area near Port Douglas. They were flown to the central distribution in North Sydney. Then it was an easy distribution to all major urban areas of Australia.

The entire operation was coordinated from St. Leonards. The business depended upon speed. Speed of transferring information and speed of transferring goods. The key was a tight data security system. That meant codes. There were lots of ways to set up codes. All code systems had flaws. Codes could be broken by competitors. Frank Bengotti and his brother Al had decided that the most secure way was to change codes often, every month. Changing codes meant delivering new sets of code indexes securely. That is why they had contracted with TRANSCOM to make discreet deliveries of new code indexes. They were encrypted into a file on a data disk delivered every two months to all major warehousing and distribution centers. They had relied on TRANSCOM carrier service because they were very discreet and trustworthy.

Frank walked into the office where Harrold Lassiter was working at the computer terminal. "What have you found, Harrold?" asked Frank.

"You're not going to like this Frank. You've been hacked into."

"Damn," bellowed Frank. "How? Who? When? Why?"

"I found eight instances. But, worse than eight instances is that in four of those instances they not only broke in but they altered your data base."

The look on Frank's face showed how stunned he was. He picked up a set of print outs and threw them against the wall sending floppy disks flying across the room. "What do you mean they altered my data base?"

"I don't know yet. It's going to take some more time. But, it looks like they did something to each of the files each time they entered. In addition to altering the files they made subtle changes in the order forms. This is not just some kid hacking in. This is sabotage by an expert."

"Keep working," replied Frank. I want to know what has happened. This could be a major threat to our business."

Frank Bengotti walked into the next room of the office with a scowl on his face. He reached for the phone and dialed the cellular number of his brother, Al. Al was somewhere in flight to Indonesia to check their supply route of plants out of the Indonesian jungle. He met with younger brother Renaldo. They did this about four times each year to cement their local Indonesian relationships and to actually go into the jungle and inspect the hillside of plants being raised for commercial distribution by the hill tribesmen. There was always some risk. If the hill tribespeople ever discovered there was more money in heroine or cocaine, they wouldn't bother raising exotic nursery stock. It was a gamble to try and reach Al by cellular if he was on board a Qantas plane. The last ring ended and Al was on the line.

"Al, we got a big problem. Harrold Lassiter is working on our computer system. We been hit."

"No, not hit by a virus. I only wish. We could repair that. We been violated. Yea, violated as in someone breaking our computer security and hacking in. No, he can't tell yet who or where from. It could be from anywhere. No, we have no idea why. While you are at the supply end, keep your eyes and ears open. Maybe you'll discover something which will help solve our problem. Talk to you later."

Frank Bengotti replaced the receiver with a long frown on his face. His mind had begun running through the list of people who might have a reason to sabotage their business. Competitors came to mind first. There were three large nursery companies who were major competitors in the tropical plant business. They were the first possibilities. Then he mentally noted half a dozen small independent operators. Maybe, but how would they stand to benefit unless they had a large source of capitol? Those small independents were in no position to pick up the business if Bengottis folded. Any personal enemies? Not here. They had a few disgruntled former family members in San Francisco. Did one of them bear a deep enough grudge to mount this kind of sabotage? No. No one. The frown deepened because Frank Bengotti was drawing a blank.

# PINE GAP

It was an unusually cool day in the center of Australia. Cool is a relative term. A 'cool' day in the center of Australia in the fall, April, means 100 degrees Fahrenheit.

A few miles outside Alice Springs, United States and Australian Air Force personnel coming on duty for the day, along with those who were completing duty, were collecting in command headquarters. The event was routine. This happened at the change of each shift. The satellite monitors and other highly secret military intelligence activities were operated jointly by the United States and Australia. There was hardly a movement of air craft, ship, or even land vehicle in the eastern hemisphere which could not be monitored by some means from this location.

Today was not routine. The discovered breech of security had been found to be frequent and not random. Military computer technicians, many of whom had grown up in Silicon Valley, had determined that the violation of security had been professional in nature. Today's briefing was to inform the new day's personnel about the status of the problem.

Majors Janetta Jackson and Frank Everhart were entering the room at the same time. Frank's wife had dropped him off on her way into Alice Springs to work at the local dry goods retail store. Like other Australian and American service spouses she became bored if she did not have some activity in the community. She worked three days a week in the store. Frank coached a 10-12 year old soccer team. It was a lonely assignment. They couldn't talk much about what they were doing there. Frank's wife had to say he was in land survey. Supposedly the Pine Gap Joint Command was a highly guarded secret. Most of the people in Alice Springs knew the secret. Most said very little about the fact. Most of the aboriginal people knew about the base. They communicated about it somewhat through their network.

Janetta, who was single, spent her spare time helping at the local youth club. She often took the same 10-12 year children on treks out into the outback for overnight camping.

"Frank, did you notice the way Nigel has begun to open up around other children?" asked Janetta.

"Yes, for the first time in soccer practice he joined a group in an organized cheer for his teammates. Until last week he was almost a recluse. What do you think happened?"

"I suspect that he has been moved so many times, he has never learned to interact with people his own age. On the camping trip last week he and two other children became temporarily lost. They weren't really in any danger. But, they didn't know that. The three of them joined together out of necessity and found their way. In the process they formed a sort of bond."

"And that has carried over into the soccer group. He's like a different lad. Now he talks and interacts with several of his mates."

At that moment the door opened and in walked all of the base brass and one stranger. The stranger was wearing an American Army uniform with a star on his shoulder. Janetta and Frank quickly exchanged glances. This was no routine briefing. The general was here for some specific reason and it was not inspection. Others in the room made similar observations. As the general approached the front, the room fell silent.

"Ladies and gentlemen of the joint command, I am General Irving Pryor. I am here because of a serious security problem detected recently at this base which may have grave implications for both the American and Australian military." He paused, dramatically. Silence in the room. Individuals shot brief glances at others in the room. After a pause of five seconds which seemed like fifteen, General Pryor continued. "As you know, data security has determined that there was a breach of security in our live communication. As you also know, further investigation has revealed a serious breach of our data bases. The full extent of the violations is still not known. The investigation is on-going. I can tell you that in all likelihood planned joint southeast Asian training operations between the United States and Australian, along with other southeast Asian forces, have been put at risk. As you know, the training exercises are intended to enhance multi-national emergency operations. Although these may be viewed by some as insignificant, that is not the case. Operation SAVE assumes a variety of crises situations ranging from natural disasters to insurgent guerrilla biological attacks. Those exercises were in phase one last month. This month phase two is to commence. Obviously someone or some group has an interest in those training exercises. We do not know who or why. The fact that there is clandestine interest is sufficient to cause the highest level of alert. Computer technicians will continue efforts to determine who and how the breach of security occurred. Once that is determined, we can then proceed to determine why."

Everhart leaned over and whispered to Jackson, "Sounds heavy." Jackson raised an eyebrow and nodded in reply.

"Each of you is commanded to note any suspicious or unusual communication occurring. If you note anything, I repeat, anything, notify security immediately. Thank you."

As General Pryor turned and exited the room everyone looked at their neighbor with a stunned look.

"Looks like a rather bumpy situation," Frank Everhart commented to Janetta Jackson. "I guess we better keep alert."

"In Texas we would say someone dumped cow patties in the front lawn. Yes, I would say this is serious. There has been a lid put on those joint training maneuvers. Supposedly it was a secret outside of the joint command and this monitoring base. Let's go see what we find today."

# WESTERN KANSAS

Unlike central Australia in April, cool in western Kansas means 45 degrees Fahrenheit. But, winter wheat is normally beginning to develop nicely in April. The rust observed by Delbert Kettering a few days ago was spreading rapidly. It was spreading two ways. It was spreading in intensity and it was beginning to appear in spots east of the original infestation. So far, only a few stalks at the original site had actually begun to wilt. That was the first step in dying. Delbert and Racheal were following every lead they could find. The gloomy spell was broken by the phone call from Cindy Nelson in Kansas City. Rachael was excited that she had heard from her college friend. They had lost touch after college. She was surprised that Cindy was still Nelson. She had been popular and attractive. Maybe she had in fact married and had chosen to keep her maiden name. That happened a lot now. So, Cindy was a lawyer. She said she was driving out with Martin White of the Kansas City Star. Was that her husband? Rachael was beginning to get excited about the visit as she prepared some cookies for afternoon tea.

Delbert was just pulling into the driveway. Rachael was glad they would have a few moments before Cindy and her friend arrived. She knew that Delbert was worried. It did not show in his becoming short or angry with anyone. It showed in his intensity of focus with anything he was doing. Losing the wheat crop would mean losing the major portion of their income for this year. Through crop diversity they would have some income; but, the wheat was the big income. They were no different than any other farmer in western Kansas.

"What is the latest crop status?" she asked as Delbert entered the kitchen.

"Still progressing. I drove around the county. It looks like the rust is still spreading. It seems to go almost like a wildfire. We have to find some solution fast. Anything new from the university or from Washington?"

97

"Nothing. The university research teams probably haven't had time to complete their second level tests. The Department of Agriculture in Washington is really dependent upon regional research like that at the University of Kansas. I checked for any e-mail just about 30 minutes ago."

Just then they both observed a car driving up the lane from the highway. Since the car was not recognized as a local car, they assumed it was their guests arriving. Rachael was excited about seeing her former sorority sister after several years. Those had been carefree, exciting years. Even though they were not close friends they had done a lot of sorority things together. There had been  fund-raisers, planning dances, studying, homecoming events and more. Rachael and Delbert moved together toward the door leading to the verandah which circled three sides of the house. They watched the new blue Taurus enter through the front gateway and pull to a stop next to the house. As Cindy exited from the car, Rachael almost ran down the steps. They met with the hugs of two people who could remember sharing good times.

"Rachael, it's great to see you again after so many years."

"Cindy, you look like life in the big city has been good."

While the two former sorority sisters were extending the excitement of their greeting, Delbert walked down the steps and shook hands with Martin who had come around the side of the car. They had already begun to become acquainted when Rachael and Cindy realized they were both neglecting social graces.

"Rachael, excuse me. I would like to introduce my friend, Martin White. Martin, Rachael Kettering."

"I am pleased to meet you Martin," replied Rachael. "Cindy and Martin, my husband, Delbert Kettering."

"Delbert and I have already met," replied Martin.

"You gals were having such a great time reliving days gone by, we just got on with it," added Delbert.

"Come in. Where are my manners" exclaimed Rachael. "You will have something to drink. Coke? Tea? coffee? wine?"

All four walked up the steps to the large verandah. As Rachael went in to take care of drinks, Delbert ushered Cindy and Martin to the comfortable rockers on the verandah. Folks in rural Kansas are friendly by nature. Friendliness to visitors is ingrained into their normal behavior as a part of their cultural heritage.

Rural western Kansas was lonely in pioneer and homestead days. A visitor who was not obviously some kind of threat was a pleasure to have. They would have been offered a cool drink and possibly a small meal. It was always a chance to get news. Visitors were infrequent. No matter how difficult the times were there was always something to serve visitors.

Rachael and Delbert were very modern farmers. They knew and appreciated modern music and literature. They surfed the internet. Their farming methods were the most modern. But, they still held and practiced some old values. Friendliness to visitors was one of the values.

Racheal had served each one their special order and joined them on the verandah. They had talked their way through the obvious. Rachael and Cindy had relived some college days and caught up on what had happened since. They relived some of the old stories of campus days. And, of course, who had married who.

Delbert and Martin had explored how each had met their significant other and explored their own college days. Surprisingly they had much in common. Both had been active in student organizations even though they had very different majors in college. Delbert had majored in agriculture economics. Martin had majored in communication and history. They both had written for college newspapers. Delbert and Rachael had two children who were old enough to help with the farming. More family was not down the road. No, Cindy and Martin were not married. They had had some long discussions. Their careers always seemed to get in the way. Maybe down the road a bit.

"So, Martin, I understand you are writing about our wheat problem," commented Rachael as the conversation shifted from two separate dyadic communications outward to one involving all four individuals.

"Yes. I heard about the problem with stem rust spreading eastward from Colorado. I knew how potentially devastating that might be for places like western Kansas. It seems to me this definitely is a problem which may have broad human interest. Just the economic impact alone would make it a major story. The impact on humans and families adds more interest. I am not trying to sell papers on the sob story of wheat farmers. But, I am interested in portraying the problem in all of its dimensions. I am also interested in being able to tell the story of how this impending crises plays itself out."

"You seem somewhat certain it will play out," commented Rachael.

"Oh, I am certain it will. How it will, I do not know. I would like to know and I would like to be able to tell that story."

"For us, we can't see the end yet either," added Delbert.

"Just how does the stem rust pose a problem to the wheat plant?" asked Martin.

"Oh, it's a fungus," replied Delbert. "The rust chokes off the flow of nutrients through the cellular/vascular structure. That causes the plant to slowly die. Dead plant, no wheat head to harvest."

"OooK," replied Martin with uncertainty in his eyebrows and forehead.

"Let me try to simplify," added Rachael. "Water and nutrients flow up the plant stem. The plant stem is like PVC plumbing pipes with side pipes off to various parts of the plant. Water and nutrients go up and the product of photosynthesis goes down. The roots send back up more nutrients to expand the upper areas. That is what we call growth."

"I understand that," replied Martin. I like your simplified analogy. I may use that. But, I thought that rust, or the fungus we call rust, develops on plants later in the year. Why so early hitting young plants?"

"Now, we would like to know the answer to that question," added Rachael. Preliminary reports from the University of Kansas researchers suggests that this is not a common form of rust. It seems to be some form which might have mutated from another form. Whatever, it is not known in the family of rusts."

"What else have you found?" asked Cindy.

"We know it is spreading," replied Delbert. "With my observations alone I can verify it is spreading about ten miles each day. One day it was started on the west side of our property. By the next day it was appearing on the west edge of another farm ten miles east. Another three weeks and it will reach Topeka, which is about the eastern edge of the main wheat belt. I don't know if it is spreading north and south as well. I suspect it is."

"Didn't you folks initiate the flurry of activity by the University of Kansas and the U.S. Department of Agriculture?" asked Cindy.

"Yes," replied Delbert. "Actually, the credit goes to Rachael. She is the internet expert. It wasn't more than an hour after I returned telling her of the problem and she was on the internet looking for information."

"Did you find any?" asked Martin.

"Not much. I found three possible hits. Nothing useful in the first two. So I contacted the university, the governor's office, and the department of agriculture. In less than an hour all three had replied. We have been busy communicating ever since."

"You mentioned three hits," Cindy added almost as a question.

"Yes, two I checked and they were not helpful. They were just generic about plant rust in general. Normally, it isn't very common to wheat."

"What was the third hit," asked Cindy. "You didn't check it. Why not?"

"It was in Australia. I assumed it would not be particularly relevant. This thing seems to be spreading through the air. Australia is a long way for a spore or whatever to travel."

"True fact," replied Rachael. "But, don't you think it might be worth a look-see?"

"I suppose it might," replied Cindy. "It certainly won't take long. In fact we should have done that originally. I guess you have to explore all the possibilities. Cindy, I guess that is why you are a lawyer and an assistant district attorney and I am not."

Martin sat upright and came to a rest in his rocking chair. All three were immediately attracted to him. "I have a college buddy who is a free lance journalist in San Francisco. Jeff Spencer is presently in Australia. You know, if that Internet item is of any potential use, I am certain I could contact him and have him check it out further."

"Martin, what a brilliant idea," exclaimed Cindy.

"Yes, I appreciate that," added Rachael. In fact, if you won't be too bored, lets go in now and we can all check it out."

Delbert was the first up out of his rocking chair. "Right this way, folks."

# SYDNEY

Aaron stepped off the escalator at Wynyard Station and into the bright sunlight beaming down on George Street. It did not take long to cross the street and go up the block, through the Strand mall, go out into Pitt Street Mall. She was meeting Jeff at the '1-2-3 Cafe.' She was hoping he was having better luck than she had. Aaron was frustrated by the fact that she had not been successful in her efforts at Macquarie University. She had followed the bottles line of investigation. It appeared to be a dead end. Hopefully, Jeff had better luck with the computer disk lead. As she stepped off the escalator and into the '1-2-3 Café' she looked through the main seating out onto the balcony overlooking the Pitt Street Mall. She spied Jeff waiting in a favorite spot next to the balcony wall overlooking the mall.

"Jeff, great to see you."

"How was the train ride across the harbor," asked Jeff.

"Quick. The trains are on time. The bus to and from the train station to Macquarie University seemed to take forever. Actually, it was on time it just seemed forever."

"And your results?"

"Zilch. They send samples of test projects for storage in Canberra. All the actual research is done at Macquarie first, results are e-mailed to wherever, and then the samples are retained in Canberra. Nothing helpful in that."

"What about the nature of the research? Any clue there?"

"It doesn't seem to be, at least at first glance."

"What exactly was the research about," asked Jeff.

"Some problem with wheat stem rust somewhere up in Queensland."

"Yes, I know about that. Actually I am researching that problem."

"Great. This might be useful for you. But, it doesn't appear to have any relevance to the murder of that poor man at the Opera House."

"Maybe and maybe not. Let's not close the book on the bottles."

"OK. Now what did you come up with regarding your angle on the computer disk?" asked Aaron.

"Nothing for sure, yet."

"You went to Bengottis? Is that the name of the company?"

"Yes. They are a national, actually international, plant wholesale and retail company located in St. Leonards. I went to their location and talked with a character named Frank Bengotti. He seemed to be the one in charge."

The waiter arrived setting down two glasses of Lindemann's Chardonay wine which Jeff had ordered. One for himself and another knowing exactly what Aaron would be wanting.

"Is he one of the Bengotti owners?" asked Aaron.

"I later found out that he is one of the Bengotti brothers. There are three of them. Frank, Alphonse, and Renaldo. They own a world wide plant nursery business. Actually they have almost a vertical monopoly structure."

"A vertical monopoly?"

"Yes, they grow plants in Indonesia, ship them wholesale into Australia, and then retail them in most large Australian cities."

"Wow. I didn't realize there was such an operation."

"Actually there are three in the Pacific/Asian region. Two large ones. There is Bengottis and there is the Wuan corporation. The Wuan corporation operates mostly in Japan and southeast Asia. They are a relatively new presence in Australia and just appearing in New Zealand."

"You found out all this from your visit to Bengottis?" asked Aaron in amazement.

"No. Of course not. They wouldn't tell me much about their business," replied Jeff.

"Sooo?"

"I got most of my information about them from an agricultural data base which I have access to through the internet."

"OK. So they are in the nursery plant business. What about the computer disk?"

"Nothing on my first visit. They really stonewalled. After I left and found out who they are and what they do I went back. It is amazing how far you can get once you have stripped away anonymity."

"You went back a second time?"

"Right. Once confronted with the fact that I knew a lot about them I think they were afraid not to talk to me. On the second visit I talked with Frank and Al both. It seems they are really worried about the Wuan's and what corporate spying they might have been doing."

"So what have you found out about the disk?"

"They finally admitted there was a disk. They insist there is nothing on it but business related information. When they found out it is in the hands of the police, they were not very happy about that."

"Do you think they are trying to hide something?"

"Oh, yea. They're hiding plenty. It may not be illegal. But, there is lots of information somewhere they do not want anyone to know about. Right now they are probably trying to figure out how they are going to get that disk back from the police."

"What else did you get from them?" continued Aaron.

"Well, it seems they use the courier company to regularly communicate information to all of their Australian wholesale and retail outlets. It seems to contain information about shipments."

"Can't they communicate that more simply by regular e-mail or fax to their outlets?" asked Aaron.

"I would assume so," replied Jeff. " I would surmise that they use some coded communication and they may need to periodically send new codes to all of their outlets."

"They told you that?

"No, I am surmising. They have to be using this means of communication for some very sensitive material. If they are afraid that competitors or whoever might intercept snail mail, e-mail, fax, or any electronic other means, then they might be

105

sending everything in code. If so, they need some way to change the codes often enough to thwart whoever they fear. If that is true, then they just might be sending new coding which can be used to interpret messages received. They would have to change those codes periodically if they really do have someone out there they fear."

Aaron stared at her drink for a moment. Slowly she looked up at Jeff and commented, "You may have it about right. Now, if you are correct, and someone wants that information, they need the disk, right?"

"Right."

"But, Jeff, why murder the courier? That poor man was just an innocent carrier. Why murder him and why at the Opera House? It had to be planned. They shot him using a silencer during the point in the music when the percussion would be the loudest. That is something which is carefully calculated by someone who knows music. Why?"

Jeff shrugged his shoulders and arms. "Beats me. Maybe he was an agent of some kind carrying a message in his head. Maybe there was something on the disk or in the bottles which he didn't know about which someone didn't want passed on. Beats me."

Aaron had a deep thought look on her face which changed in intensity with each of Jeff's suggestions. "I don't think he was an agent. He didn't look or behave like the type."

"What do you mean he didn't look or behave like the type. He was quiet, unnoticed in what he did. He was the kind who blended into any crowd of people; like at the horse races, or at the symphony concert at the opera house. Sounds to me like just the type for a good agent," replied Jeff.

"No way. No way," affirmed Aaron in a voice which claimed definitive knowledge.

"OK, if not the agent theory then how about the innocent carrier theory? He was carrying something he knew nothing about. Zap!! He was erased. Happens in all the good movie plots, right?"

"Right and wrong. Right. It happens in movie plots. Wrong. This is not a movie plot. This is real life. And real death! Who would be using him to transmit secret information? The government? No way. They have powerful secret satellite communication hookups with your U.S. governmental armed services. They have better ways of sending highly secret information."

"But, how do you know it wasn't some other government or terrorist group which doesn't have such powerful communication means? And, what about corporate espionage? Suppose some corporate competitor needs to get information transported secretly? Why not encode a message within an already supposedly secret message? It's like piggybacking. No one knows."

Aaron was listening with a face much blanker than before trying to sort out Jeff's speculations. "OK, for the sake of theoretical speculation lets assume you might be on to something with your 'corporate sabotage transport information theory'. Now why kill the poor man? Why slaughter your own carrier pigeon?"

"Wow! I like your metaphors." Jeff shifted from his left elbow to his right elbow and leaned into Aaron. Suppose they wanted the disk, planned to get the disk and couldn't find it before the concert ended? They couldn't begin frisking the poor corpse as the concert was ending and lights in the opera house were coming on. Now, does that give my 'corporate sabotage transport information theory plausibility'?"

There was a prolonged silence. Seconds passed as Aaron stared into Jeff's eyes as they sat face to face, inches apart. Suddenly her hand flew around his neck and she kissed Jeff hard. "I think you may have something," she exclaimed.

"I sure do. I just got one hell of a wake-up kiss. Almost spilled my drink all over," he replied wiping up spilled wine on the table.

"Sorry, I got carried away."

"Fine. I am just glad I have such an effect on you right here in the middle of the day."

"Well, of course you do. Always. But, I was struck by the impact of your logic. I think you may be on to something. But not just the 'corporate sabotage theory.' Your logic also works for the 'terrorists planting information theory' as well."

"Thank you," nodded Jeff.

"Now, if you are correct, then the disk must have something deeply encoded in the message."

"Can you get the disk," asked Jeff.

"Why?"

"I know a guy in Manley who is a computer nerd. He can find anything if it is there," replied Jeff.

"Are you sure? How can he find something the police haven't."

"Believe me he can find it. Can you get a copy from the police?"

"I don't know," replied Aaron.

"I'll bet you can. Call that Lieutenant 'what's-his-name.' Make him get you a copy."

"How can I 'make' him get me a copy?"

"The police know your reputation for solving murders. They don't like to admit it. But, they already have."

"What do you mean?"

"Remember. They are already 'feeding' you information through your assistant. If they are doing that, they want your help; but, they don't want to admit it too publicly."

"So, how do I convince Lieutenant Wilson that giving me a copy of that disk will help them solve the case in some way they can't?"

"First, if they could solve the case they would have done so. They haven't. In fact we probably know more than they do already. They probably already know that too. You call Lieutenant Wilson and get him down here. When he gets here you tell him you think there is secret information on the disk and you know someone who might be able to decipher what is there."

"What if he refuses to come?"

"Tell him you have information about the case. Tell him to be here in thirty minutes."

"Do you think he will come?"

"He'll be here in twenty minutes."

"And if he comes?"

"Tell him just enough to tease his appetite. Then tell him your expert will decipher whatever is hidden in the disk. When he hesitates, you assure him that you will share anything you find before you run a story and that he will get all the credit when you do run your story."

"OK. We'll give it a try."

Twenty-two minutes later Lieutenant Wilson stepped briskly up the stairway to the '1-2-3-Cafe.' The fact that he was slightly out of breath revealed that he had hurried from the police station. As he approached, Aaron rose to meet him. Jeff sat back with a self satisfying "I-told-you-so" smile.

"Thank you for coming so quickly," greeted Aaron. "I know how busy you are. We appreciate your time."

"Well, hopefully we are all after the same objective. Murder at the opera house does not set well with Australia's modern reputation. And, it's on the worldwide news. I suppose the Herald takes credit for that."

"Sorry, Lieutenant. We were holding off one edition. CNN had it on their worldwide feed. Within minutes Britain's Sky News had it on. Actually we were scooped!"

"Lieutenant, did you bring Aaron a copy of the disk?" asked Jeff.

"Sorry, I can't do that. That evidence can not go out of the station."

"I really would like to help. In fact I believe that we have access to some computer expertise which would help you with the case. If you can't let me have the disk, there isn't much I can do to help," argued Aaron.

Jeff continued to sit back smugly in his seat listening to the apologies of Lieutenant Wilson and to Aaron's pleas to let her help. After the exchange had gone on for almost five minutes, Jeff decided to chime into the exchange. "It seems to me there is a perfectly easy solution to this impasse which seems to be preventing judicial progress."

There was silence and sustained stares from both Wilson and Aaron. Finally after what seemed like an eternity of silence, Aaron broke the spell of silent stares. "What do you mean by that Jeff?" Wilson added an agreeing nod.

"What I mean is that there is a solution. Aaron, you have a reporter intern assigned to this case. She has been working through the police among other sources. Lieutenant, you have found it convenient to allow the Herald's intern to be able to 'pry' information out of one of your young detectives assigned to the case. You have been feeding Aaron information by that means so that she can follow up on leads which would perhaps not be appropriate or quite legal for the police to investigate."

There was silence. Aaron had a shocked look on her face. Wilson had a stunned look on his face. Wilson spoke softly and slowly and asked, "How did you know?"

"How could I not know?" replied Jeff. "It is obvious where Aaron has gotten some of her information. It is also quite obvious that you knew she was getting the information. It is not a stretch of the reasoning process to conclude that you approved of her getting the information. I am just suggesting that you continue the same communication link. Ratchet it up one notch."

"I can not part with that disk," Wilson barked, clearly annoyed by the fact that Jeff was on to his game.

"No worries, Lieutenant. Keep the disk. Just tell your young man who seems so infatuated with Aaron's intern from the Sydney Herald to make a back up copy of the disk and give her the back-up disk the next time he gives her a box of candy. He can just put it in a plastic bag right inside with the chocolates. Aaron will have the disk within the hour. Then we can get it to an expert who can work on searching for any coded information. Simple?"

Lieutenant Wilson just stared for a few seconds. Then, a smile began to creep along the left side of his mouth. "What makes you think you have a source who can do any better than our own experts?"

"We have such an expert available," replied Jeff. Just see that the disk gets to Aaron. I'll see that it gets to an expert. If we find anything helpful you will be the first to know Lieutenant." Jeff leaned back even further in his chair with a satisfied smile on his face. Aaron shot him a wink of acknowledgment.

"OK. But, remember Aaron, this is confidential information you are getting. If I see it in the Herald before it gets to me we will be at war."

"No worries," replied Aaron with a huge smile and an extended hand to 'shake on it.'

Lieutenant Wilson shook her hand, nodded toward Jeff and walked away.

*George E. Tuttle*

# SYDNEY

It was a cool day in greater Sydney. That meant it was pleasant to be out walking about the city. Jeff had taken the train across the harbor. He was sitting outside at a cafe in St Leonards trying to figure out why they had not been able to obtain any useful information from the Bengottis. They had resisted cooperating until virtually forced to give information. Jeff was wondering what they were hiding. Were they the link in this murder investigation? He had picked up the computer data disk from Aaron's intern from the Sydney Herald, Jennifer Cross. Jennifer had gotten a call within an hour from her young policeman contact at the police department. It was amazing how quickly an 'unofficial' exchange had been arranged. Jennifer got it to Aaron who got it to Jeff who in turn got it to his friend at WEB Data International.

WEB Data International was a home operated international company located in a Yuppie's home in Manly. The company was actually located on the second floor of a small used bookstore in Manly across the street from Manly Beach. William Edward Barclay IV was the owner and operator of the international data service located above the bookstore. William Edward Barclay IV, WEB, of WEB DATA INTERNATIONAL did not work above the bookstore. But, his dozen or so 'twenty-five something' employees did work there. WEB worked two blocks away out of the second floor of his own home. He was connected electronically with his business. This was his 'office.' He went to the business workplace above the used book store every Friday afternoon to socialize with his employees before they headed for the beach or whatever. He did not really need to go to the business workplace. All the important business was handled over the internet or on a secured closed line satellite connection. WEB went to the business just to socialize. He understood what was missing with the use of electronic technology—the REAL human contact. So he went to socialize.

112

Jeff had done a lot of work with WEB. He had worked with him electronically from various parts of the world. When he was in Australia, he worked with him more person to person. They enjoyed a good rugby match now and then. Jeff had taken the disk to WEB's home and asked him to search it for any hidden messages. WEB had asked what he was looking for. Jeff said he did not know. Supposedly, the disk contained commercial information relating to the nursery stock business. Was there anything hidden in the data? Was there anything coded in the data? Was there any data masked by compression of part of the data? Anything? Jeff knew that if there was anything to be found, WEB would find it. Now, Jeff just had to wait for WEB to contact him.

When Jeff met with WEB, Jeff had been given a message which had arrived from his newspaper contact in Chicago. Even though Jeff was a freelance writer, he had a mail box located at the Chicago Tribune. Jeff had an arrangement to have his mail opened, scanned and forwarded to him when he was out of the country. It was a nice courtesy because of the fact that the Tribune really appreciated the great stories he filed with them. The message had been a fax from his friend, Martin White, with the Kansas City Star.

Jeff was mulling over the message he had received from Martin. It was asking him what he knew about a strange plant disease in Queensland, Australia which may have been reported. Martin had said in his message that he was there working on a major story about an unusual plant rust epidemic in Kansas. He had information that an internet story had been filed out of Australia about a similar epidemic in Queensland. In Kansas the rust seemed to be effecting wheat. It spread very rapidly. Could he find out anything about it? Jeff recognized immediately that the case referred to by Martin had some similarities with the story he had been investigating.

# PINE GAP

Operations at the secret Australian/United States communications base at Pine Gap outside Alice Springs were normally quiet, smooth, efficient, very high tech. This was not the usual bustling military base. Even though most local people knew the 'secret base' was there it seemed almost invisible. The military staffs functioned so quietly and efficiently at work and in the community where they worked and lived it seemed more like a quiet conservative insurance headquarters than a military base. That is what both countries wanted.

What actually took place was remarkably intense high tech communication. Much of the watching of earth circling satellites was actually seen here first, and then in Washington and Canberra. Much of the coordinating communication of military activities was occurring here. With the United States the major military presence in the northern hemisphere and Australia the major military presence in the southern hemisphere, monitoring of worldwide communication and coordinating of activities was controlled here and in Colorado Springs, Colorado. The joint activities by the military of both countries at the Pine Gap Base was a remarkable testimony to the American/Aussie alliance.

Once the world's flash points were mostly in Europe. Now they were more often in southeast Asia. Indonesia, the Asian subcontinent, the various island groups were far more dangerous as flashpoints than any other region. Therefore, it was only logical that longtime allies like the United States and Australia who both have vital economic, social, and political interests in the broad Pacific Rim would develop coordinated military ventures.

Pine Gap had originated as a joint communication venture during the early days of the Vietnam era. It also served well to monitor United States satellite orbits. Now, Pine Gap was a major communication center. It monitored satellite imaging. It coordinated highly secret military exercises between the

American and Aussie forces. It kept close track of activities throughout southeast Asia. If there were to be need for United States, Australian, or joint action in any area of southeast Asia, Pine Gap would be the communication hub of both intelligence and operations.

Because of all these reasons, there was great concern for potential damage from computer hackers. Usually they were harmless teenagers proving to their handful of friends what they could do. The young nerds were not a real threat. But, they had to be stopped before they inadvertently did serious damage to on going exercises by carelessly damaging databases.

Majors Janetta Jackson and Frank Everhart had been working overtime, along with military security personnel. General Pryor had been making frequent visits into the operations room asking quietly if any progress had been made in identifying the persons who had repeatedly hacked into the data bases. Pryor was making another of his strolls through the beehive of activity.

"Results?" asked General Pryor.

"Some results," replied Jackson. "We have been able to narrow the location of the origin of the security violations to the Indonesian region. We are still working on a pinpoint."

"Anything else?"

"Yes, general," replied Everhart. "It appears that some of the violations are red herrings."

"Red herrings?"

"Yes sir, we have detected six violations into relatively minor data bases."

"Such as?"

"Payroll records, weapons descriptions, the like."

"How do you determine they are minor?"

"The categories plus the fact that there is only one violation per category. Finally, these six were the first six we located. It appears they were assuming we might find some violations, note these as insignificant and not raise a general alert."

"And what about the violations which were not red herrings?"

"They are serious," replied Jackson. "It is clear there are at least a dozen. Six in each of two categories. The two categories are joint training exercise related data bases and satellite control category."

"Those are indeed serious categories," comment General Pryor.

"More than just the fact that the categories are serious," added Everhart. "Six violations in each category. In both sets the progression of the violations is a pattern."

"And what is that pattern?"

"First, just an ordinary hack in, just like in the ones we call red herrings. Then from the second through the sixth violation, each entry goes deeper into the data base. In both categories, the last, or sixth, violation appears to be setting up a planted virus which might be programmed to take over control of the data in the data base."

"That means it might be possible to generate false data to impact upon the progress of the training exercise and to move the satellite pattern so that it might miss a normally planned region of surveillance," added Jackson. "If it is done skillfully, the 'planted bug' could divert a satellite temporarily, return it to its proper line, and hide any trace that a diversion had occurred."

"So someone might want to temporarily divert our attention and then execute some kind of maneuver, perhaps coordinated with our scheduled training exercise?" Pryor stated as a question making a statement out loud.

"I think that is a possible conclusion," offered Everhart.

Jackson nodded agreement and Pryor asked, "anything like this previously?"

"We are not certain.," replied Everhart. "I have some vague recollection of a similar pattern about nine to twelve months ago. It will be necessary to check records of prior hacking entry instances."

"I already have it up," added Jackson. "There is a parallel situation exactly 182 days ago. The problem was analyzed then and unresolved but attributed to teen-age hackers. I think we can do a more complete comparison and we may find a significant relationship."

"Carry on," commanded General Pryor. "Good work. We need this resolved ASAP."

"Yes sir," both Everhart and Jackson replied.

# SYDNEY

Aaron and Jeff had spent the previous evening at the Opera House. It was the first time they had been back since the murder occurred. This morning they had each gone their separate way following up leads. Aaron had returned briefly to the Sydney Herald to take care of important tasks which could not be delayed. She had also talked at some length with Jennifer Cross, the intern following up on the murder story about Stanley Hutch at the Opera House. Jennifer had done two background stories which she by-lined with Aaron.

Aaron and Jeff had arranged to meet for lunch at the rose garden in the Royal Botanic Garden. It was a favorite spot for both of them on nice days. Today was another warm day with a light breeze off the harbor.

Jeff was sitting under their favorite gum tree overlooking the rose garden. He was just taking in the striking beauty of the Royal Botanic Garden. He had picked up their cheese, bread, and wine for lunch. Jeff knew that he and Aaron were committing a lot of their time to the murder case. He was also trying to commit some time to the puzzling e-mail message he had received from his colleague at the newspaper in Chicago which ran a lot of his by-line stories. He had asked Jeff to investigate an agricultural wheat problem in Kansas which seemed to have striking similarities to a wheat problem in Australia. In addition to that Jeff had his own research and writing to complete. He knew that Aaron had her own work at the Herald. The murder investigation was a time stealer for both of them. All of that meant less time for them to spend together. How many times had they been to the Opera House? Once since the murder. Terrible. Normally they would be there three or four times by now. They needed to get this case solved.

"Hi Jeff," announced Aaron as she swept down the hill to join him at his bench above the rose garden. "What a beautiful day. Wonderful breeze off the harbor, roses in bloom, warm sun. I could stay here all afternoon."

"Right on everything except staying here all afternoon. But, lets enjoy what we can."

"So what have you found out about the disk," asked Aaron.

"Nothing yet. My friend, WEB, has not gotten back yet. Or, maybe he has and I have not been in my room to get his message. But, I have gotten an e-mail message from Chicago."

Aaron looked at him with a raise eye brow. Since she was busy taking a bite into her cheese, it was all she could do to communicate her desire to know what it was all about.

"There is some sort of agricultural plague sweeping across Kansas and my friend has been contacted by another friend, Martin White. It seems Martin thinks there might be some link to some problem which was sweeping through the Darling Downs down here."

"And why did they contact you," asked Aaron as she finished her cheese and was ready to take her first bite out of the fresh loaf of bread they were sharing.

"It seems there was a story on the Internet about it. They thought maybe I might be able to check it out. It really is similar to the story I just wrote but haven't submitted yet," replied Jeff as he began pouring their bottle of Wolf Blass Chardonnay."

"Similar in what way?" asked Aaron.

"Similar in that wheat is involved in both cases. Beyond that I am not sure. Some time today I should get an extended e-mail attachment with Martin's story. Then I can see just how similar. Even if they are similar, that doesn't mean they are related. So, what have you found?" asked Jeff as he began his cheese and bread.

"Jennifer Cross has been pursuing several angles. First, she got some good information from her source with the Sydney Police."

"You mean from her source there that Lieutenant Wilson is using her to feed selected information?" asked Jeff.

"Well, its a bit more than that. Yes, they are using the source to 'leak' selected information to her. But, the source doesn't realize he is being used that way. So he is actually giving her more information than Lieutenant Wilson or anyone else intended."

"And?"

"And, the police have done a complete forensic sweep of the victim's home. They have discovered several interesting things. First, they have some fingerprints."

"That's not unusual. He must have left plenty and he must have had guests."

"Not too many guests according to interviews with neighbors. Yes, they found lots of his prints. They also found at least three other sets of prints at various places around the house."

"Could they identify any of them?" asked Jeff.

"One set made a hit in the print data bank."

"Really, who was it?"

"Not a nice person. The set belonged to Stephen Wuan."

"And who is Stephen Wuan?"

"Stephen Wuan is a notorious international gangster best know for various suspected illegal activities in Indonesia, Malaysia, the United states, and Australia."

"Oh really," Jeff commented as he poured more wine.

"Yes, really," replied Aaron. "Several arrests in all four countries but only minor convictions. But that was enough to get his prints into the data bank."

"What kind of arrests?"

"Assault, drugs, speeding. They finally nailed him on speeding with a small quantity of drugs. He got probation and left the country. Obviously he is back. None of the assault charges could stick. It seems that subjects in several countries just would not testify or just disappeared."

"Sounds like a not so nice guy."

"Right. The police theorize that he and one or more others were actively searching his room. It could have been for that disk. It could have been for the bottles."

"Do the police think they might be connected to his murder," asked Jeff.

"They think it is likely. Apparently they think he and the others were searching for something after he was killed."

"OK, but why was he killed at the Opera House during a performance?"

"The police aren't sure, but they think it may have been to eliminate him. The murderers fully expected to get what they wanted from his jacket at the time. That points to the disk rather than the bottles. He did not have it with him. They beat it out to the Opera House and made it to his home before the police did."

"But, why? What was the motivation?" asked Jeff.

"There they are stymied. They still do not know. Here is the last of the cheese."

Jeff took the last piece of cheese and handed Aaron the last of the bread. They sat back, enjoyed their food, finished the wine, and watched three sail boats drifting by the Botanic Garden. Three sail boats is a quiet day in Sydney Harbor. On most nice days the harbor is filled with various crafts. It is said that one in every three Australians living within 100 miles of the coast has a water vehicle of some kind. By mid afternoon the harbor would probably be filled.

Jeff and Aaron sat silently for a long time. They just savored the quite beauty of the harbor and the Botanic Garden. Birds glided silently through the trees. The ever present gallahs broke the silence from time to time with their noisy calls.

The moment was prolonged until Jeff reached for Aaron's hand and said, "I hate to break the magic spell but what are we doing this afternoon?"

Aaron thought a moment and replied, "I must be at the Herald for a 1:30 meeting. Then I want to go back to Bengottis in St. Leonards. There has to be more information to be found there. That is the company which engaged TRANSCOM to

121

transport their disk to Canberra and then to other sites. I want to know more about Bengottis, TRANSCOM, the disk, and how they all tie to someone wanting to murder poor Hutch."

"OK," replied Jeff. "You pursue your angles. I need to get with my friend, WEB, and find out what he has discovered about the disk. I also need to try and follow-up this story on a possible link between wheat rust in Kansas and some similar kind of wheat problem they had down here in the Darling Downs. There might be a connection."

They got up to leave. Aaron was dropping their paper refuse in the trash container when she abruptly turned and grabbed Jeff's arm. "Jeff."

"What is it?"

"No it couldn't be," Aaron paused and stared at Jeff.

"Aaron, what is it?"

"Is it remotely possible there is some connection between your story and this murder?"

"How? They don't have any connection that I can see."

"Yes there is," Aaron blurted. "Jeff, yes there is a possible connection. Hutch, the poor fellow murdered. Who did he work for?"

Jeff was silent. He was thinking. Then his face changed from bewilderment to awareness. "Yes, you are right."

"TRANSCOM," they both shouted at each other simultaneously.

"Aaron, you may have something. He worked for TRANSCOM. In that job he was the carrier of a disk involving Bengottis and he was the carrier of those bottles containing samples of the lab analysis done at Maquarie on its way to Canberra. Both disk and bottles were going to Canberra. Wait a minute. This is too much. We don't know there is a connection."

"And we don't know that there isn't a connection," replied Aaron. "Jeff keep it in mind. It just might be a connecting clue. See you tonight for the concert at the Opera House."

Jeff and Aaron embraced, kissed, and were on their separate ways.

# KANSAS

Rachael and Delbert Kettering had gone their separate ways after breakfast. They had enjoyed their visit the day before with Rachael's college sorority sister, Cindy. The discovery that they had so much in common after so many years and such different paths to their lives was interesting. They had renewed their former friendship in only minutes. They reminisced for hours into the evening after supper which had deepened their friendship.

Rachael and Delbert had tried to get them to stay over. They argued that they could continue their investigation into the wheat stem rust problem together into the night. Cindy and Martin could not stay. Cindy had to be in Kansas City to make early morning appearances at her office and in court. Martin wanted to work out of his newspaper office. Cindy and Martin had arranged, though, to return the following day which would be Saturday. They would then be able to stay over to continue their friendship and to continue pursuing the wheat stem rust mystery.

After breakfast Delbert had driven out into the county to check his own fields and those of neighbors to the east, which was the direction the stem rust seemed to be spreading. It was clearly an airborne substance following the prevailing winds. As he drove through the county roads he was seeing more and more signs of stress.

Delbert arrived at a neighbor's field just to his west. He walked over to the field and checked some plants near the outer edge. Four out of five plants were infected. Two plants out of every five were almost lifeless. Perhaps they were beyond repair. The rusty appearance on the stem was a sign that the remaining plant cells were infected with chemicals from the dying cells. For some reason the fluid distribution system was shut or shutting down. The decaying cells had a reddish coloration. Thus, it appeared rusty.

Delbert walked further into the field, stopping every few yards and studying a sample of five plants. He was finding the same results no matter where he walked among the plants. He made his way back to his truck to drive over to another neighbor's field further to the east. He expected to find the same problem just beginning to appear in those fields. That is just what he found. It was depressing to find such rapid spread of something unknown destroying the crops. He felt absolutely helpless.

Rachael had returned to some household chores, doing some data entering into their financial records, and then turned to checking the internet. She wanted to check the website in Australia which had the third item which had been brought up by her web browser when she made her original search on the internet.

Rachael connected with and downloaded the third stem rust story. And she was stunned. The similarity of the problem being reported and discussed in the story from a site in Australia was so eerily similar to the problem she and Delbert were facing. The site was somewhere in the Darling Downs region of Queensland, Australia. Rachael knew that Queensland was a northern state in Australia. She also knew that part of the state was highly agricultural and that wheat was one of many agricultural crops. She had read enough reports of world crop estimates to know that it was a region which grew a lot of wheat; and thus, was a major competitor with Kansas wheat in the international market.

Now, someone there seems to have had some kind of wheat stem rust problem which had been sweeping their crops. Rachael did recall an earlier report last December that there were some problems with the wheat crop in Australia. World prices had risen for brief period of time. She and Delbert had even briefly considered the idea of speculating on the market. If they had committed to a futures price at that time, they stood to make a substantial profit on this year's crop when the crop was delivered. Now she was thankful they had resisted the temptation. If their crop did in fact fail they would have had to deliver thousands of bushels of wheat they would not have. Then they would have to buy those bushels of wheat on the market themselves at the prevailing market price. It could have ruined them. That would have been worse than a bad year's crop. This instance reinforced the conservative approach she and Delbert took to agriculture economics and production.

Rachael continued reading the story she had downloaded from Queensland. It reported that the crop had not been a total failure for everyone. Only for some of the early victims. It appeared that some kind of cure had been found in time to save a good portion of the Queensland crop. That explains why the December futures market had been affected only for a few weeks. The saving of much of the crop had restored estimates of production which in turn lowered the market price.

At that moment she heard Delbert driving in. She saved the downloaded file so they could read it together and figure out what it meant for them in Kansas. As she finished saving the file Delbert came into the house.

"Rachael, that rust is just continuing to spread," announced Delbert as he walked into the room. "It has now infected over 60 percent of our fields. Some of the first infected plants are showing so much moisture loss stress they may not survive anything we can do. Other properties in the county look as bad or worse."

"I may have a little bit of good news," replied Rachael as she walked up and threw her arms around Delbert.

Delbert reached around her and gave her a big long hug. They kissed. "I appreciate any little help," replied Delbert. "But, we need a lot of help. And we need help quick."

"Delbert, we may just have a lot of help. I could kick myself for not checking that third site when I checked the internet for stem rust. That third story is so similar to our situation it is eerie."

"Really!"

"Yes. Really. That third item is about a wheat stem rust problem last December in Queensland, Australia. I just finished down loading and reading part of the story. When you drove in I saved the story so that we could read it together."

"Well, what are we waiting for?"

# SYDNEY

Police Lieutenant Wilson was waiting in his office at police headquarters on George Street. He was waiting for a visit from two Americans. He had gotten a call about an hour before from the United States embassy. It was an unusual call from the Assistant Ambassador. He had been asked if he would meet with a representative of a Unites States agency. There was no indication if who or which agency. He agreed and the Assistant Ambassador indicated they would meet him at his office in an hour. Wilson found the entire matter unusual. He had asked his Captain, Randall Smithfield, to be available to meet with them. He was not certain if this was something for which he wanted to be solely responsible.

The door opened and three men and a woman entered the room. One man was tall, over six feet four, dressed in diplomatic style. One of the shorter, stockier men stood about six feet and exhibited  military body language although he was not in uniform. He was ramrod straight. His color was black. The other short, stocky male was about six feet one and also exhibited military body language. But, he was in uniform. He was in the uniform of the Australian Army. The female was about five feet nine inches. She was well dressed and also exhibited a hint of military. "Lieutenant Wilson?" the tallest man asked.

"Yes. I am Lieutenant Wilson."

The tall man extended his hand and stated, "Pleased to meet you. I am Assistant  United States Ambassador Henry Adams. We talked on the phone about an hour ago."

"Yes," replied Wilson.

"Lieutenant Wilson, let me introduce Frank Morgan and Cynthia Edwards."

They all shook hands and extended greetings.

"Please. Everyone be seated." Wilson pulled five chairs around the table in the room where he often worked. "And what can the Sydney Police Department do for you Ambassador? I presume you are from the United States."

"Yes, most of us are," replied Ambassador Adams. "However some of our roles go beyond just the United States. Colonel Morgan..."

"Frank," interrupted Morgan.

"Frank," continued Adams, "is with United States military intelligence; but, he is currently on loan, so to speak, with Interpol for a special assignment which we want to discuss with you. Ms. Edwards..."

"Cynthia," interrupted Edwards.

"Cynthia," continued Adams "is an agricultural researcher with the University of Kansas; but, she is on loan, so to speak, also with Interpol. Cynthia is also formerly with the United States military Far Eastern Command. And, finally Mr. Ragsdale..."

"Scott," interrupted Ragsdale.

"Scott is a member of the Australian Armed services. Scott is with Australian military security. All three of the guests I bring you are here on a very important security matter. I believe all of these connections will be relevant to our discussion. Lieutenant are we in a secure room?"

"If you mean is it totally soundproof, no. But, the walls are not thin and we do periodically check for electronic bugs. We are relatively secure. May I suggest that since what is appearing to me to be a matter of some consequence that it might be well if my Captain were to join us."

"No problem," replied Adams. "We quite expected you to ask. May I caution, though, that at this time our discussion is quite sensitive and the number of people involved in the loop should of necessity be quite limited."

"No worries," replied Wilson as he rang for his superior. "For now we can keep the loop small."

Seconds later the door opened and a uniformed officer entered. All rose from their seats at the table. As Wilson made the introductions he pulled another chair to the table. The six were again seated as the introductions and admonitions for limiting the size of the loop of knowledge were repeated.

"Let me begin briefly," said Ambassador Adams. "It seems that there may be a security threat to both Australia and the United States with some possible connections here in the Sydney area. Scott will you continue?"

"Thank you Ambassador. We have reason to believe there is a person in the Sydney area who may be involved with or have knowledge of an operation which threatens the security of both nations, possibly with worldwide implications."

"Here?" asked Captain Smithfield.

"Yes, we have intelligence that he may be in this area," replied Scott Ragsdale.

"You mentioned a serious plot, Scott. How serious and how is the person you seek involved," asked Lieutenant Wilson.

"We have evidence of a breach of military data security systems. The investigation of that breech has led us to investigate a plot to spread plant disease viruses among worldwide competing nursery stocks," explained Scott.

"You mean someone wants to kill plants and that somehow involves the murder of the poor guy in the opera house," asked Wilson. "Why? What is the connection? How does that threaten the world?"

"Colonel Morgan... Frank. Would you explain," asked Ambassador Adams?

"Yes. It seems that the 'poor guy' was not quite what he seemed. Our joint investigation has revealed that he is connected with the operation as a carrier of information. He carries computer data disks, along with other unrelated items. The computer disks contain mostly cursory stock inventory information including shipping information. Suppressed within the data are other sets of data. These suppressed sets of data are important."

"What kind of suppressed data?" asked Captain Smithfield with a wrinkled brow.

"DNA information," replied Morgan.

"DNA," exclaimed Wilson and Smithfield. "How can that be computer data?"

"Yes, DNA," continued Morgan. "It is plant DNA. The chemical structure of certain DNA chromosomes has been mapped. By manipulating one or more components of the strand it is possible to make a radical change in the life form which evolves. In this case a plant life form."

After a moment of silence Wilson and Smithfield exchanged puzzled glances. "I am still at a loss to understand the threat from a computer data and a plant's DNA," said Wilson with a wrinkled brow.

"Let me try to establish the scientific link for you Frank," offered Cynthia Edwards. "Then you give them the reason why we are here." Colonel Morgan nodded. "DNA is actually composed of microscopic bits of protein and acid building blocks. They can be represented in an on-off switch fashion. That is how computer data works. So, if someone wanted to transmit how to construct, reconstruct, or slightly modify some life form they could communicate that by computer data. Scientists communicate with one another regularly in that manner. But, it is possible for one to hide the communication in such a way that: either someone else can take it and use it to modify existing structures; or, perhaps even more ominously, let the data be buried in other data along with computer data commands which would cause it to take over some existing robotically controlled growing system."

"What you're saying Ms Edwards—uh Cynthia," interrupted Smithfield, "is that someone could control what happens to a plant simply by hiding data on a disk?"

"Precisely," added Edwards. "It can be transmitted electronically or by hand carrying data stored on a floppy disk."

"Why use a floppy disk and involve a person?" asked Wilson. "Wouldn't it be easier to send it over the internet?"

"Not necessarily because there is a small risk of interception over the Internet no matter how much care might be taken. A person carrying an apparent harmless disk is less risky if you can be certain you trust the person carrying the disk."

"Which brings us to why here," interjected Morgan. "The Australian and United States joint security teams have determined that someone from the Sydney area has been hacking into and altering military data files."

"How is that linked with plant DNA manipulation?" asked Smithfield.

"The link is that they are accessing highly military anti viral research which is often transmitted through highly secured means," replied Ragsdale.

"You mean it was secure," interjected Wilson.

"Precisely. Nothing is ever 100 percent secure. But, our communications are indeed highly secure. Secure enough that our research scientists use the systems for highly classified communication. In this case we have been able to determine that someone in or near Sydney has been using the military communication to change the nature of communicated DNA data. In so doing they have been able to spread a plant virus which could be highly dangerous."

"How is it dangerous?" asked Smithfield.

Everyone looked toward the plant research expert, Cynthia Edwards. She look at Ragsdale who nodded before she spoke.

"The joint Australian and United States research team has been experimenting with a variety of jungle plant species to locate potential antigens for biological and perhaps even chemical warfare. We had been focusing on some plant types in tropical and subtropical regions. Most promising were some species common to higher regions of Indonesia and in the northern rain forests of Australia. We had considerable success in finding substances which will serve as antidotes to known biological and chemical agents. In several instances we have altered the DNA structure of certain species to produce an even more useful antidote material. Those plants are maintained in a highly secured region."

"Are those plants dangerous?" asked Wilson.

"Not directly in and of themselves," replied Edwards. However we have observed that with only slight modification in the DNA structure of those plants they produce a plant which emits a viral waste product which can be highly deadly to certain other types of plants."

"What kind of other plants?" asked Smithfield.

"Many of our commercial agricultural grain crops," replied Edwards.

The silence in the room was stunning. Wilson and Smithfield looked at each other, at the others, and then again at each other again in disbelief.

"Back to your question about why here," continued Morgan from Interpol, "We have determined that the center for communication activity is in this area. Based on that we speculate that the center for the operation may also be here. We so far can only speculate on motive."

"And what is your speculation about motive?" asked Wilson.

"At present our speculation is that someone is trying to create a threatening terrorist situation. Perhaps some sort of international blackmail might be the objective of the operation."

"So, what are you asking of Sydney Police?" asked Smithfield.

Ambassador Henry Adams had been sitting back listening as the discussion had progressed. At this juncture he leaned forward and spoke in answer to Smithfield. "I believe that it is important for Australia and the United States, perhaps even much of the world, for us to  support the efforts to quietly terminate this potentially threatening operation. I say quietly because if it became widely known to the media, there might arise a panic among the public. For that reason we need to keep our discussions as secure a possible. I believe that  Colonel Morgan—Frank—can speak to what help your force can provide."

"Thank you Ambassador," interjected Morgan. "We need to have access to any records you might have of anyone, group, or company dealing in any way with agricultural or plant products which might have a criminal record even if they have not been prosecuted or convicted. We would be most interested in any which have had any international connections or dealings."

"That sounds like a lot of searching," interjected Wilson." "We can do some searching of records but it will take some time."

"We have some expertise available which might make the search quicker," replied Morgan.

Wilson looked at Smithfield and replied, "I hesitate to open police files to outside agency searching. We would be happy to cooperate as much as we can and conduct whatever search you might suggest."

Scott Ragsdale had been sitting back listening to the flow of the conversation. At this point he sat forward, opened a file of documents, and spoke. "Let me add to my role as member of this investigation by establishing my credentials with the Australian Military Command. My letter of designation from the Prime Minister and Department of Defense empowers me to take any necessary steps as member of the Austrialan/ United States Joint operation to protect Australian national security." He passed his folder to Wilson who read carefully and passed it on to Smithfield.

Smithfield read the folder containing the two letters carefully. He sat for a moment, looked at Wilson, and then spoke to Wilson and to Ragsdale. "Given the unusual circumstances and your national security authority, the Sydney Police Department will make any records open to you as you wish. I might add that it would probably be helpful to you if one of our staff assisted as they search the records."

"Yes indeed," replied Morgan. "We can have two joint security officers here within ten minutes to begin work. We consider this to be of the utmost importance."

With that, they all departed from the room to set in motion a most unusual cooperation between Australian and United States military as well as local Australian police officials. There had not been such a close cooperation of national and local authorities since during World War II when General MacArthur was headquartered in Brisbane. The close cooperation had continued through the turbulent 60s, 70s, 80s, and into the 90s. Both the United States and Australia had common interests all around what had come to be called 'the Pacific rim.'

# ST. LEONARDS

The Bengotti brothers had been in a state of anxiety for the past few days since their computer engineer had determined that their data bases had been compromised. They immediately sent secure messages to all their retail outlets in Australia and to their supply center in Indonesia.

The first message to the supply outlets was to alert them to the fact that insecure messages had been distributed. They were asked to make wire phone contact immediately if they noted any unusual shipment in the past few weeks and if they noticed anything unusual in the next few days. Further, the retail outlets were made aware that a new security code system would be sent to each of them immediately by confidential snail mail. The new security system was to be operative in five days. Until that time they could not order or receive any shipments. To the brother Renaldo and his suppliers in Indonesia they had sent a message explaining that the security had been compromised. Renaldo was ordered to fly to Sydney the next day and obtain further instructions. In the meantime no shipments were to be made until further notice. Any electronic contacts with the supply center were to be noted and reported. No reply to the source of any contact was to be made.

A day later the two brothers, Al and Frank, were seated around a table in the back of their office flanked by Harrold Lassiter and their brother Renaldo who operated the supply center in Indonesia. Lassiter had data output sheets spread in front of them on the table. He was explaining what he had been able to discover to that point.

"Here is what I have found so far," began Lassiter. There have been three kinds of penetrations of our security. The first type of penetration has altered distribution data."

"In what way?" asked Al.

"In a few cases the orders have been changed. Then, in a few additional cases the shipments have been altered."

"Wouldn't our retail outlets notice?" asked Frank.

"Not necessarily," replied Lassiter. "The changes were so small they would hardly be noticed. One plant here, two plants there. That sort of thing"

"So someone gets an order for one too many plants or someone receives one less plant. Is that what you are saying?" asked Renaldo.

"Exactly," replied Lassiter. "No one is likely to notice one plant short or one plant too many. The breaches of our security system is so minute and insignificant it slips by routine checks. But, what puzzles me is the fact that in three cases the changes were made and then they were reversed before they could be executed."

"You mean like someone changed their mind?" asked Al.

"Maybe. Maybe someone wanted to establish a pattern of entry and exit without consequence so that it would go unnoticed. Then at a later date they might use that route to do something more significant. I do not know the motive. I can only describe what has happened to the data."

"You said there were three types of security breaches. What are the other two?" asked Frank.

"The second type of security breach is the placement of some spurious data into our data system," replied Lassiter.

"What do you mean spurious?" asked Renaldo.

"I mean data which I can not interpret. I can read it but I do not know what it means. It is like some kind of scientific code which I do not understand."

"Harrold, I thought computer data was all bits; as in on and off," said Frank.

"It is. However, all those on and off bits eventually take on recognizable characters which can eventually be read by some program as language. All I can determine is that these are raw bits of data. They have no language meaning to me."

"How often did you say this type of security breach has occurred?" asked Al.

"It has happened at least three times," replied Lassiter. "The first was last spring. A second time was this fall. The third time was just last week. There does not seem to be a pattern to the three incidents."

"And the third type of security breach?" asked Frank.

"The third type of security breach was very specific in nature. It took control of one of our plant research sites in Indonesia." Lassiter looked to Renaldo and asked, "have you had any unusual problems with research this past year?"

"None that comes to mind. We have been doing some routine testing of several plants to determine which ones might be best suited to adapting to the various climates south of the tropical region." Renaldo looked puzzled as he spoke to Lassiter and then to each of his brothers. "How could someone be messing with what we are doing that in the fields and controlled temperature green houses up there?"

"I'm not sure," replied Lassiter. " But I am sure of one thing. Someone has put some strange type data into at least three sets of data going into your center."

"Where is it coming from?" asked Frank.

"Somewhere in the Sydney area."

"How can you tell that?" asked Al.

"By the unique computer signature trail left by whoever was inputting the data," replied Lassiter. "Let me explain it this way. Every single computer in the world has an identification number buried in its BIOS. When someone goes into your data over the internet, they leave a trail containing that identification number. I can locate the number. By knowing some of the manufacturing patterns I can determine approximately where that computer is probably located."

"You mean a computer leaves a trail like a fingerprint?" asked Al with amazement on his face. "I though everything with computers could be made highly secret and that guys like you can make them secure."

"Only in a relative sense," replied Lassiter. "The dirty truth is there is no such thing as a truly totally secure computer, either receiving or sending data. By searching I found the ID and determined that it came from this general area. What I do not know is what the nature of the information is which was sent through the data. If I can have you think back to the research you do in the Indonesia source center, together we might be able to figure out what it might be."

"OK," said Renaldo leaning forward on the table with both hands opened. "First we get an idea of the conditional growing limits of various plants. If they look promising in terms of appearance, ease of care, etc. we subject them to some DNA changes to see if we can enhance or prolong their life. Sometimes what we want is to change their cellular life system in order to make it easier to transport. Perhaps we want them to retain moisture longer or perhaps we want them to retard growth at certain stages. If we can manipulate some of those variables we have a plant which has a commercial edge over our competition."

At this point Harrold Lassiter was sitting back looking puzzled. "You mean you can alter a plant just like that?"

"Yes, it is a technique I learned in my agronomy studies. We do quite a bit of it up there. We are isolated enough that no one is going to be nosing around about what we are doing."

"I hate to ask," interjected Frank, "but is this legal."

"Yes, it's legal where we are. It can't be traced in the plants which come in because they are all natural at that point. Naturally we don't let our failures out of our greenhouses. There are some people who have some ethical problems with how we change DNA. But, it's legal. No one is going to jail over this practice."

"Let me ask," queried Harrold Lassiter, "are the data you keep on plant experiments kept in data files?"

"Yes, it is," replied Renaldo.

"And further, are the manipulations of plant DNA or environment or anything else controlled by automated processes which are turned on or off by computer programs?"

"Yes, they are."

"OK. There you are. Someone is inputing data which does things to your plants which you do not know about."

There was stunned silence as the three Bengotti brothers stared at Lassiter, at each other, and back to Lassiter.

"OK, lets get back to identifying the trouble for our operation in Australia," interjected Al. "Where is this coming from? Harrold, you said it was someplace in the Sydney metropolitan area. Where?"

"As I said, I do not know the precise location. If I ever had physical access to the computer from which this signature came I could locate it inside that computer."

Frank Bengotti leaned forward, looked slowly at each person and said, "I have a pretty good idea." There was silence. Each one silently stared at Frank. Their silent stares were saying 'well go on, tell us.' "I think it is the Wuans," stated Frank.

# WESTERN KANSAS

Delbert and Rachael Kettering were standing arm in arm along one of the wheat fields near their home. They had been walking the rows looking at the wilting plants. These were wheat plants about six inches tall. This was one of several critical points in the growth stages of the wheat plants. Many, in some cases most, of the plants had a reddish brown appearance to the stem. What this meant was that the cellular structure was clogging up and could not transport nutrients to the plant. The plants were in effect starving as well as dying of thirst. Very little water and almost no food nutrient could flow up the stem. Now they stood for a long time at the end of several rows. They both looked dismayed by what they had been seeing. As they had walked along the rows they had checked some of the plant roots. The roots were healthy appearing but seemed unable to push water and nutrient up the stem.

"It begins to look hopeless," said Rachael. "Is all of the crop this bad?"

"Some is this bad and some is almost as bad," replied Delbert. "Overall I would say that at least fifty percent of our crop is in this state or worse. Another thirty percent is almost as bad. These plants we are looking at are still alive but just barely. But since we do not know what is causing this rust we have no idea what, if anything, can be done."

"We heard from Martin White today via e-mail. He is in touch with his journalistic friend traveling in Australia. He is asking him to check out the details of the item we found on the internet about a similar rust problem on wheat in the Darling Downs region of Queensland, Australia. Maybe they found something which can help."

"I hope we find out quickly. Another few days and these plants will be beyond recovery even if we do discover anything."

"Lets go inside and try to reach Martin again. Maybe he has heard something."

Delbert and Rachael walked slowly up the pathway to the modern farmhouse. Just as the prairie settlers sod house once gave way to the square farmers home of the 1870s and 80s today the square home after one or more additions had given way to a modern brick ranch home with all of the modern conveniences. Delbert and Rachael were modern farmers and they had a lot in their life to lose if their crops failed. As they walked into their office and signed on to the internet there was the sound of a car coming up the driveway. Delbert looked out the window of the office and saw Cindy Nelson and Martin White drive up.

"Rachael, here come Cindy and Martin. Just the people we were talking about." Rachael and Delbert made immediately for the front door. After a round of pleasant greetings they made for the cool comfort of the gazebo in the back yard.

"Del and Rachael, I think Martin may have some encouraging information for you," said Cindy.

"I hope so," replied Rachael. "We need all the help we can get. That wheat is dying."

"I have located my friend, Jeff Spencer," said Martin. "He is in Sydney Australia doing research on, of all things, agriculture. He plans to do a major piece from 'down under.' What I have done is let him know that we are in contact. It seems that there may be some real similarities between what is happening in Kansas this spring and what happened in Queensland during their spring, which would have been last September and October here in Kansas."

Del and Rachael's long looks changed to anticipation as they looked at Martin.

"That item you found on the internet from Queensland was checked out by Jeff. It appears to be the same problem that you are experiencing here in Kansas and in eastern Colorado. It seems that there was a problem in the Darling Downs region and it was solved before the crop was lost. Not all of the crop was saved but most of it was saved. Most important, the spread of the disease was stopped. I do not know the details but Jeff is investigating his story to see what help there might be for you."

"That's the best news we have heard in a long time." exclaimed Rachael." She was the first to express the relief that was on her face and Delbert's face. "Is there anything we can do to speed this process along?"

"Maybe," replied Martin. "I understand you are on the internet. Let me share with you what I received from Jeff. I will also give you Jeff's e-mail address. It might help you to be communicating directly with him."

"This is terrific," said Delbert." This calls for a drink of celebration."

"Don't celebrate too much too soon," cautioned Rachael. "But a small cool drink is warranted. Lemonade or wine?"

"A white wine for me," replied Cindy.

"Same for me," added Martin.

"All the way around," added Delbert. "Cindy, let me get the wine. You are the computer person. Why don't you get the addresses. And, I think we should share this information with the agriculture experts at the University of Kansas in Lawrence. If we have any hope of applying any suggestions we will want their input into the matter."

After sharing recent travel experiences as they sipped their wine, Cindy and Rachael went into the house to Cindy's computer to make a contact down under. Martin and Delbert remained at the gazebo discussing the whole course of the crisis.

Martin had made it clear to Delbert that he was doing a newspaper story and anything he was relating might appear in the story. For Delbert, that was not a problem. He knew the importance of the media in communicating to the general public. He knew too well that for too long people in agriculture had been leery of the media. In many cases with good reason. But, he knew that if farmers expected to have sympathy and even support from the general public the general public had to know and understand what problems faced the farmers. This rust situation was a potential crisis for the nation. He wanted to help Martin in his effort to put together a truly useful, informative story.

# SYDNEY

Jeff Spencer and Aaron Worthington had two things which continually brought them together. They shared a lot of cultural interests like music, opera, good food, the museums and history of their respective countries. This was an interest which brought them together every time Jeff was in Sydney, Aaron was in San Francisco, or they were both at some location at the same time. Their relationship was strong but for nine or ten months out of the year physically separated by 12,000 miles.

In addition to shared cultural interests, Jeff and Aaron were drawn together emotionally in solving some unusual and complex puzzles. They seemed to relish tackling some highly public puzzle in a quiet way. Always, they saw that legal officials, police or whatever, received the spotlight and the credit for solving the puzzle. Aaron's name appeared in print only as an editor of the Sydney Herald. Jeff's name appeared only as the author of some interesting scientific or agricultural story in one or more newspapers around the world. Only a small number of police and government judicial enforcement agencies knew who they were.

More than once Jeff and Aaron had joined forces to investigate murders or missing person cases which had baffled the police. That had happened twice in Sydney, Australia, Once in San Francisco. And a third time in London. Their unique access to information without the restraints limiting police official investigations led them to sources which ultimately allowed police to make an arrest or to resolve a missing person case. Also, there had been two cases in Australia when their investigation resources had enabled them to uncover financial fraud. Again, they had means which were not limited by official legal constraints. In one case known only to Sydney New South Wales fraud investigators they had uncovered evidence which enabled authorities to arrest and prosecute. Jeff and Aaron had done so by indicating to authorities where and how to look for the needed evidence. In one case, the evidence was buried deeply in computer data files.

Among Jeff and Aaron's resources was the assistance of several people who helped them. One was William Edward Barclay IV, a computer expert, who was able to find incriminating evidence in data files in a case involving financial fraud. How he had entered the corporation's data banks was not totally ethical but not quite illegal. He passed the information along to Jeff and Aaron who in turn passed the information along as a source protected tip to authorities.

It was this same William Edward Barclay who was helping Jeff and Aaron unravel what was on the copy of a data disk which had been 'obtained' from police. He had easily found the obvious variant data in the disk. But, he felt that was not the essence of the embedded information. What he found initially was just a bit of data directing the shipment of goods to locations which did not fit with other distribution data. It was just a few cases. But, that is why it was so obvious. What Barclay, WEB as he was known to Jeff, theorized was that there was more information more skillfully embedded in the data. In reality, it was probably codes with codes within normal data. It was just like cracking the World War II German 'super code machine,' Enigma. Barclay was working on teasing the deeply hidden code out of the disk.

Jeff and Aaron were having lunch at their favorite spot, The '1-2-3 Cafe,' in the Pitt Street Mall in downtown Sydney. They sat at their favorite table on the balcony overlooking the shoppers on the mall street below. Jeff had just finished a Chook Pot Pie and a light mixed salad. Aaron had a bowl of Irish Stew in a bowl of bread. They were both finishing their wine, a Lindemann's chardonney. They had been discussing the chamber music they had heard the night before in a small theatre in the Opera House.

"Jeff, let's review what we know, what we suspect, and what we need to know," said Aaron. "First, we know that this poor fellow was killed in the Opera House during a performance.

Second, we know that he worked as a delivery person. Third, we know that at the time he was shot he had material he was to transport for two clients."

"We suspect that one of the two may have had some motive to kill him," added Jeff. "We suspect that the reason may be something on the computer disk he was carrying or in the bottles he was to transport to Canberra."

"We know that one of those clients, the Maquarie University, had no reason to have him killed. They were just sending bottles of research material for storage at the Commonwealth Agriculture Repository in Canberra."

"Right, not unless someone did not want those bottles to arrive."

"We have no inkling of why or who might have an interest in the bottles. I would rule that one out as a suspect," concluded Aaron.

Aaron and Jeff both paused to think. It was an opportunity to pour another glass of wine. They swirled the wine lightly in the glasses, letting the aroma escape and fill the upper part of the glass.

"Further, we know that the Bengotti Brothers of Bengotti Nursery Imports were the source of the computer disk the victim was transporting," continued Jeff. "And, we know that the Bengotti brothers are less than forthcoming with information."

"Right," added Aaron. "It was only after we threatened them were they willing to volunteer anything."

"We know that the police have not found anything of interest to them on the disk. The fact that they 'allowed' us to obtain a copy for analysis establishes that fact. But, I think there is something there."

"When will you hear from your 'computer wizard' friend?"

"I hope later today," replied Jeff.

"Can we speculate about that disk? It may simply be corporate data secured against competitive corporate espionage."

"That is a possibility," replied Jeff. "Even if corporate espionage is the explanation, it could still lead to a motivation to kill the data carrier. Corporations will sometimes go to ultimate lengths to protect themselves."

"Or, it might be a vehicle for hiding some information of an even more sinister nature," continued Aaron.

"Like what," asked Jeff.

"Like... Like, maybe some terrorist group using an innocent mode of communication to transmit its own information or to trigger some devilish plot."

"Now you are really engaging in wild speculation," commented Jeff as he nearly spilled his wine laughing. "Wild theories like that and you wonder why the police are suspicious of letting 'civilians' be involved in solving criminal mysteries."

"Wild theories like that are what sometimes will solve criminal mysteries," asserted Aaron. "How do you think I have been able to help the police solve so many cases. Someone has to engage in wild speculation. The police can't and won't do that. I will. Sometimes I am right."

"And, often you are well wide of the mark," replied Jeff. "But, but for the sake of good conversation along with good wine I will indulge you. More than Lieutenant Wilson will do. OK. Proceed with your 'terrorist plot' theory."

"Well, I can't go much further until we have some hard information. Like from your friend. But, it just might be something like this. Some international terrorist group has developed a poison of some kind."

"What kind of poison?" queried Jeff with a wrinkled brow.

"Don't editorialize on my observation with your wrinkled brow," snapped Aaron. "I do not know what, if any, kind of poison. But, it MIGHT be some kind of poison."

"Go on," encouraged Jeff with a straight face and another sip of wine.

"Maybe they have some kind of poison which they want to transmit or send. They might want to send it along with regular plant shipments by a company like the Bengottis. It would make a good cover. Then, maybe, at a later date they send information which is trigger information which somehow triggers a release of the poison. Very subtly the poison begins to spread and does terrible things."

"What terrible things," asked Jeff wrinkling his brow again.

"Stop that! There you go again editorializing about my theory. I do not know what 'terrible things.' I don't even know if this is what happens. Remember? I am engaging in wild speculation. Indulge me without editorializing!"

"OK. OK. Really, I was just thinking the kind of doubts you could expect to get from Lieutenant Wilson. I do see where you are trying to go with your theory. But, I am still a doubter."

"OK. Doubt! But, hear me out," continued Aaron.

"But, why murder the data messenger?" asked Jeff more seriously.

"Aha. You are beginning to take me seriously. Perhaps because he served his usefulness while the terrorist group was experimenting with whatever their terrible poison is. Now they want to take more direct control of the distribution of information."

"But, I still say, why kill the messenger," asked Jeff.

"Perhaps so they can put their own person into the loop. Maybe they have someone ready to take on the task with the courier company. Maybe that someone has applied for a job and been hired. He or she, a mole, is now ready to take over this task."

"Really speculative," commented Jeff.

"That's what we are doing now. Speculative? Yes. Very speculative. And, very possible. Jeff, you went to Bengottis to check on the disk. You said they admitted sending the disk. I think we need to know more about what might be on Bengottis' data disk. Not just this one disk but others as well. My speculation tells me that something more is there."

"So, what are our next steps?"

"Next we go back to Bengottis and see what more we can squeeze out of them. And we both need to go. Two of us working as 'good guy/bad guy' might get something more than we have so far. We need to shake them up a bit. You were the 'good guy' before. You pursue the angle that you are looking for information to enhance your story of plant rust up in the Darling Downs of Queensland. I will be the 'bad guy.' I will use my 'connection' with the police to  squeeze the information out of them."

# ST. LEONARDS

The Bengotti brothers had been busy for hours. Al was running the business and checking inventory records, invoices, and any document he could find. Frank was sitting next to Harrold Lassiter as Harrold was at the computer trying to further analyze the extent to which they had been hit by hackers and what effect, if any, it had on their shipment orders of plants. Renaldo was at another computer sending an e-mail to their research lab in Indonesia to get a detailed description of the DNA research they had been doing with plants at the transport distribution site. Renaldo knew that what they were trying to do was make some gene changes which would do several things.

First, the longevity of the plant would be extended by slowing down decay of the cell membrane wall decay. That was possible by manipulating some enzymes. One little change in the plant DNA would regulate the enzyme controlling cell decay. Result? Plants would last twice as long as the typical plants shipped by competitors. Increased customer satisfaction. Naturally decreasing the enzyme would have the opposite effect.

Second, another little change in DNA made it possible to reduce the adverse effects of shipping plants. On the same chromosome as the gene regulating the enzyme for cell decay was another gene which regulated another enzyme which changed the tolerance of dryer air which was an inherent part of the air shipment process. Air shipment was the way the Bengottis were able to obtain faster transportation. Competitors, like the Wuans, had to rely upon fast boats. Fast boats were still slower than air shipment.

All three Bengotti brothers were working as hard as they could to find out who was trying to infiltrate their business. They wanted to know if the infiltration had already happened. Further, they wanted to know what the effects were going to be.

The door opened with a jingle as Aaron and Jeff entered the outer office. Al came out of the inner office to see who had entered.

"Can I help you," asked Al in his pleasant customer voice.

"I hope so," replied Jeff. "I am Jeff Spencer. I was here the other day asking about information related to a disk you shipped with TRANSCOM Courier service. Do you recall?"

"Yes, I do," replied Al in a more cautious and less friendly voice. "What more can I do for you?"

"I hope a great deal more," replied Jeff. "I want to introduce my associate, Aaron Worthington. Ms. Worthington is with the Sydney Morning Herald newspaper."

Aaron and Al Bengotti exchanged glances as they formally shook hands. Aaron's look was formal and businesslike. It had that nonverbal message of 'no fooling around, let's get down to business.' Al Bengotti's look conveyed the nonverbal message of caution.

"Do you recall reading about Ms. Worthington?" asked Jeff. "She has been identified in several celebrated police cases for her help to the police in assisting them solve some very tough cases."

"Yea, maybe," replied Al cautiously. He wasn't too certain but he knew that it might be true. Certainly he wanted to proceed with caution in dealing with Ms. Worthington.

"So, again, what can I do for you?" asked Al Bengotti as he noticed that Aaron was moving to the other side of Jeff. The effect was to flank Al. One on each side. It made Al feel uncomfortable already. One was on his left the other on his right. He was surrounded. It brought feelings of alarm from his Vietnam experiences.

"I am doing a feature story on some plant diseases in agricultural crops up in Queensland. The courier who was killed at the Opera House had some bottles which were important to the story I am developing. Since the same individual was carrying your disk I was wondering if there might be some information you could share with me which might enhance the story I am writing." Jeff was being very outgoing in asking Al Bengotti for help to put him at ease.

"I don't know of anything that I can add. Our disk just contains inventory and routing records. It would not have anything on it about the plants other than the plant names for shipment purposes."

"Nothing at all?" asked Jeff in a near pleading voice.

"Nothing. Just dates, numbers, destinations."

"Have you had any computer anomalies?" asked Aaron in a sharp voice. It caused Al to turn sharply with suspicion. His facial look conveyed the alarm he was experiencing. Aaron caught Jeff's wink unnoticed by Al Bengotti indicating Jeff's marking the alarm in Al's nonverbal behavior. "Yes," continued Aaron. "What kind of computer difficulty have you been experiencing?" After Jeff's communication with her, Aaron had turned the question from the general 'anomalies' to 'what kind.'

"We are having some normal glitches," replied Al Bengotti in a very hesitating voice.

"What kind of glitches?" pressed Aaron in her bulldog tone.

"You know, just ordinary glitches."

"Are you losing data?" pried Aaron.

"No. Not exactly. Well, I am not too certain exactly what but we have had some strange things appearing."

"A virus perhaps?"

"Not that I know of."

At this point Frank Bengotti came into the room. He was wondering if Al needed some help with a customer. As he entered the outer office he stood just behind Al.

"Any problem Al?"

"No problem Frank. Mr. Spencer and Ms. Worthington are here inquiring about the disk carried by the courier for TRANSCOM who was murdered in the Opera House last Sunday. They wanted to know if we had any computer problems. I was just explaining that we had some ordinary glitches. Right, Al?"

"Yea, just routine stuff."

"Let's cut the crap," snapped Aaron. Her voice echoed in the room. Al and Frank Bengotti looked stunned. "We have already established that you are having interruptions in your data. How many? When? Any additional data you don't normally have?"

"Hey wait a minute," replied Frank. What right have you to come in here prying into our private business? Are you the police?"

"Let me try to be helpful," replied Jeff who had moved further to the left flank. Jeff was leaning back against a file cabinet. "Maybe I can help us look at this calmly." This was the 'good guy' Jeff speaking. "Ms. Worthington does work with the police. In fact both of us are trying to help them on this one." Jeff leaned over an casually pickup the telephone. "May I dial Lieutenant Wilson directly and ask him to verify our role?"

Aaron kept a stern straight face as she contemplated Jeff's bluff.

"No. Let's not do that," replied Frank. "We don't need police involved. We were just worried you might be working for one of our business competitors. We do have to be careful. OK. What can we tell you?"

"Back to my original questions," replied Aaron. "Give us some specific answers."

"I will tell what we know," replied Frank. Unfortunately we don't know too many details. Our computer expert is working as we speak. It seems we had some hackers get into our data bases. He tells us they have done some damage with our data."

There was a long pause. Aaron maintained her stern face continuing her role as 'bad guy.'

"Might I ask what kind of damage," asked Jeff from the left side. His face was warmer maintaining his 'good guy' role.

"You're not going to print all this?" Frank asked Jeff.

"My first goal is to help solve a very serious case. Whether any of this fits in with any story I am writing still remains to be seen."

"OK. Wait a minute," replied Frank. "Let me get our computer man. He is in the back working to see who has hacked in and how much damage they have done."

While Frank Bengotti was out of the room, Al Bengotti was explaining some of the scope of their nursery business to Jeff and Aaron. Aaron maintained her stiff stern manner just listening. Jeff was more engaging interacting with Al about the scope, transportation methods, and how they used the courier service for their business. After about five minutes Frank Bengotti re-entered the room followed by a second man.

"Folks, this is Harrold Lassiter. He is our computer expert. Harrold this is Mr. Jeff Spencer and Aaron Worthington. I have just briefed Harrold on what you are seeking."

"How do you do," said Lassiter. "So far I have found ten illegal entries through our computer security. There may be more." Al and Frank exchanged frowns as they realized that was more than he had previously told them he had found. Aaron, listening and watching, noted their surprised frowns. "I have made some detailed analysis of three of the illegal entries. There have been some changes in the data bases to which the hackers gained entry."

"What kind of changes?" asked Aaron.

"Two kinds in both instances. One kind in one of the two instances. In the first case the changes are changes in the directions for shipping locations. In the second case the changes are also for directions for shipping locations but also some kind of added information in the chemicals used to maintain steady air and moisture in the shipping containers."

"What does the change in chemicals for shipping mean?" asked Aaron.

"Beats me," replied Lassiter. I just noted there were changes. I don't know what those changes might produce."

Aaron and Jeff exchanged knowing glances as their minds began to work in harmony.

"We have a friend who is presently analyzing the disk found on the Opera House murder victim. He is a very sophisticated computer expert. Any objection if we get him up here to look at your violations to see what he can make out of the new data? He is not going to be working for any competitor. I can assure."

"What can he do that Harrold Lassiter can't do?" asked Frank. "Harrold is a good expert. Who is your friend?"

"His name is William Edward Barclay IV," replied Jeff.

"WEB?" exclaimed Harrold Lassiter.

"Yes," that is how he is commonly known. He runs a business in international data services.

"You know this guy WEB?" Al Bengotti asked Harrold Lassiter.

"Oh, yea! WEB is a legend! Most real computer experts in Australia and New Zealand learned what they know from WEB. I once took some work with WEB. I would take his help anytime."

"Then it's settled," said Aaron moving toward the group. "Jeff, you go get WEB here immediately. Harrold, you let me look over your shoulder while you continue whatever analysis you are doing." It was more than clear to all that Aaron had taken charge. No one objected.

# WESTERN KANSAS

Delbert Kettering was standing alongside one of his fields of wheat. There had been an inch of rain which fell gently during the night. Normally that would have brought a smile to Delbert's face. But, he only looked at the plants beginning to wither and die along the west side of the field. Rain would not help plants which were being strangled by some poison which was a product of the bio-cellular process which was going on inside his wheat plants. Delbert understood the general process. He just did not know the specifics of how this apparent rust was devastating his crop.

Rachael drove up in their Chevrolet pickup truck, parked, and came over to join her husband. Rachael had been working all morning at the computer. She had been in touch with the agricultural experts at the University of Kansas, the United States Agricultural Research Center, and the Governor's Office in Topeka, Kansas. She had also been pursuing the suggestion offered by Martin White, the Kansas City Star reporter, and his friend Cindy Nelson. When Rachael had commented about there being three items she found on the internet about a wheat rust problem they suggested that she should not overlook the item from Australia. They suggested it might be worth a look. Actually, Rachael was somewhat encouraged by her communication with Australia. She had read the story. It sounded like it might indeed be a similar problem. She located an e-mail address of a person at the Australian Agricultural Services Station in Toowoomba, in Queensland. So far she did not have a reply. She was hoping to get one soon.

"Delbert, we aren't licked yet," said Rachael as she moved beside Delbert circling her arm around his waist.

"It is beginning to look very grim," replied Delbert. "These plants along the west side of the field can never recover even if we knew what to do this very moment. It will only be a matter of days until the remainder of this field is too far gone for hope.

Other fields a few miles away won't be far behind. Even if we find something soon which can stop this process, the yield will be way down. Anyway you cut it, this looks grim."

"I have a bit of good news. Do you remember there were three items on the internet about wheat rust?"

"Yes, I remember. Two of them were just about ordinary stem rust. They were really old news."

"Right. Well, the third item was filed from Australia."

"In Queensland as I recall," replied Delbert nodding.

"And, I took Martin and Cindy's advice and checked that item. We should not have overlooked that. It is a report by the Australian Ministry of Agriculture reporting on something which sounds very similar to what we are experiencing right here."

"Really," replied Delbert with interest. "How old is the story?"

"Well, its several months old. But, remember their growing season is the opposite of our growing season on the calendar. So about six months ago they were faced with a kind of rust which sounds much like what we have. They found some way to halt the spread. The report does not contain all the details of the materials used to halt the spread nor does it say anything about the cellular process which took place. But, something they tried worked. And, they were able to harvest a partial crop."

"Why didn't we hear anything about it in our ag commodities report?" wondered Delbert.

"Maybe because it only reduced their overall crop production. Remember that there is also a lot of wheat grown in Western Australia out near Perth. If they had a good crop in Western Australia the national average would not have been dramatically lowered. Thus, the story might not have made it into the worldwide commodities reports."

"OK. That is encouraging. It is the only encouraging news we have had lately."

Delbert and Rachael got in the truck and headed back down the road Delbert had walked. He had been checking fields along both sides of the road for over a mile from the house. On the way back they discussed how they would proceed next.

"Also, I got an e-mail from Martin White. He has been running his series of stories on the wheat rust and its threat to the food supply. He has had two articles in print now. They are being picked up and syndicated around the country. Even around the world. He is getting requests from his publisher for more follow up. He is coming out today to take some pictures and to do some more follow up interviews with us. He may want to also interview some of the other wheat farmers. I expect him to be arriving soon. I think we should help all we can."

"I agree," replied Delbert. "Anything he can do to stimulate researchers to find a solution is well worth the price of publicity."

As Delbert and Rachael were going from the truck into the house Martin White's car was driving up the lane from the county road. Martin waved as he was parking. Delbert and Rachael were waiting for him on the verandah as he got out and approached.

"Martin, good to see you again," hailed Rachael. "Cindy is not with you?"

"No she would like to have come along but she is knee deep in a case in court. The judge has been giving her a hard time. She did not dare ask for any postponement. But, I appreciate your willingness to see me again."

"Let me get some lemonade," said Rachael. "You two sit here on the verandah. I will be right back."

"Delbert, Rachael indicated you would probably be willing to let me shoot some photographs and give me some more insight into what is going on. I would like to do another story in this series."

"Yes, we can do that," replied Delbert as Rachael brought lemonade and joined them on the verandah. "Take all the pictures you like. I will be glad to do anything which you think might be helpful. My hope is that your series of stories might trigger someone who has information or can find information about a solution to come forward."

"OK. Let me begin by asking how rapidly the rust infestation seems to be spreading."

"Well, it is showing up about ten miles per day. But, I suspect that when we get the westerly winds off the Rocky Mountains it probably gets carried further faster."

"Any word yet on how it seems to do damage to the plant once the rust spores take hold?"

"We do not know exactly. The plant and agronomy researchers at the University of Kansas are certain it is a bio-cellular process. Some agent gets into the cell structure which does not belong there and interferes with normal cellular activity; or, something blocks an important nutrient or enzyme from moving between cells. Either of those scenarios could cause the cells to produce the rust we are seeing and to basically kill the plant by shutting down the stem. It could even be something which changes the rate of enzyme flow."

Martin was becoming more and more aware that Delbert was not the stereotypical wheat farmer. He was highly educated not only in agriculture but in biology as well. Martin had not interviewed this kind of farmer before. And, in reality, the intelligent highly educated farmer like Delbert was the kind of person who was making a success in agriculture today.

"You told me it would have far reaching economic aspects," continued Martin. "I read some of the data you provided on the impact of wheat on the American and the world economy. Isn't it likely that if this rust is limited to the United States it will do serious harm to the United States economy but not necessarily to the worldwide economy?"

"No, I think it will make an impact worldwide. The world production regions outside the United States are unstable, except in Australia and Canada. The Russian and Ukrainian production is not reliable. Brazilian wheat production is not as great as their soybeans. Asian wheat is increasing but not sufficient to pick up a large market gap. Besides, the Asian production is also unreliable."

"And," added Rachael, "if this wheat rust spreads to other parts of the world that would make the problem worse."

"Speaking of Australia," replied Martin, "I still have not heard from my colleague who is down there. I am trying to get him to check into that lead you found, Rachael, up in Queensland. I have a call to him as we speak. He has an answering service where he is staying down under but they haven't been able to get him to respond. I can not figure out why he is so busy he is out of communication. That is not like Jeff Spencer."

"Actually I read the article we talked about," interjected Rachael. "I was just beginning to tell Delbert about that a few minutes ago while we were out in the field." Martin's ears perked up as he was most interested in what she had found. "It seems that in the Darling Downs region of western Queensland they have had a similar problem with some kind of stem rust. It had a negative impact on their production. However, somehow they found a solution which saved part of the crop. I printed out a copy of the article for Delbert to read. You may read it as well."

"Yes, I would like to see that," replied Martin.

"And I sent a copy as an attachment to an e-mail to the University of Kansas Agronomy Research Center. Apparently they were not aware of this item. It might be helpful to them to pursue their own research."

"Great, I will check with them when I return to Kansas City. Well, if you will help me find some people who might share their insights then I will shoot some photographs and be on my way back to Kansas City."

"Delbert why don't you take Martin to talk with the Olsons and the Bjornfelds?" suggested Rachael. "I am certain they would be helpful if you asked. I will see what more I can find on the internet. And, I need to do some financial records."

*George E. Tuttle*

# SYDNEY

Aaron Worthington was exiting the underground tube at Wynyard Station. She was headed for the Sydney Herald building. She was going to take time to make a quick stop at her office before meeting Jeff at Police Headquarters. After leaving the Bengottis she and Jeff were headed for the St. Leonards tube station when her cell phone rang. The call was from her assistant at the Herald. There had been an urgent message from Lieutenant Wilson. The message was more like a command that she AND JEFF join him at Police Headquarters immediately. Aaron told her assistant to call Lieutenant Wilson back and let him know they were on their way as fast as the tube would allow. In fact, Jeff had gone on to the next station to make a quick trip back to his room. Aaron was making a quick trip into her office before walking over to join Jeff in front of Police Headquarters so they could arrive together. She was wondering what this was all about. It was unlike the Lieutenant to issue commands to her. They arrived simultaneously at Police Headquarters on George Street.

"What do you think this is about?" asked Jeff as they started into the building.

"I don't know. But, it must be something about the murder at the Opera House. Nothing else I can think of. Maybe something is about to break," she replied as they approached the information desk. There the attendant recognized Aaron and pointed them directly through to Lieutenant Wilson's office.

As Aaron and Jeff entered Wilson's office they were struck by the fact that quite a number of people were already in the room. They seemed to be sitting and standing around chatting about various things. As soon as Aaron and Jeff had entered the conversations stopped. Everyone seemed to look first at them and then at Lieutenant Wilson. Aaron and Jeff exchanged quick glances.

"Lieutenant. We came as soon as we got your message," said Aaron. "Is something big about to break?"

" I am not sure," replied Wilson. "I do appreciate your responding. We do have an important matter on our plate before us. It is very possible that you and your associate may be able to help us."

"First, let me make some introductions. Aaron Wilson, the Sydney Harrold, and her friend, journalist, Jeff Spencer. Aaron and Jeff, you know captain Smithfield. We have several other people here who are part of this discussion today." They nodded recognitions.

"Aaron you may know Police Commissioner Nigel Davenport," continued Wilson. "He will be sitting in as an observer of our discussion."

"Next, let me introduce Assistant Ambassador Henry Adams. Mr. Adams is here in his official capacity with the United States. Then, meet Colonel Frank Morgan. Colonel Morgan is with United States military intelligence on loan to Interpol. Then, Cynthia Edwards. Ms. Edwards is an agricultural researcher here as a member of Interpol and of her government's delegation. Finally, Scott Ragsdale. Mr. Ragsdale is with the Australian Armed Services." All shook hands. "Please be seated."

Aaron and Jeff selected seats opposite each other in the middle of the rectangular table. Lieutenant Wilson sat at the head and Captain Smithfield beside him. Aaron and Jeff knew they were not in the 'power seats' at this table. But, their selected positions would allow them to exchange nonverbal communication with each other easily.

Jeff was impressed by the fact that there were high level officials from Sydney police, the military and civilian government officials of both Australia and the United States. He and Aaron exchanged raised eyebrows to indicate their feelings recognizing the importance of this group by its members.

"Lieutenant Wilson," interjected Aaron. "With such a room full of official people perhaps you would like for me to contact

Jonathan Ticehurst, editor in chief of the Sydney Harrold. Certainly if this is any kind of official business involving the Herald he would want to be present."

"Not really necessary Aaron," replied Wilson. I have asked you here in your capacity as one who occasionally helps the police with important matters. I don't believe the Harrold is directly involved."

Jeff noticed that Colonel Morgan and Captain Smithfield nodded agreement. Jeff and Aaron exchanged glances which conveyed they shared recognition that this was indeed high level but very off the record.

Aaron broke the silence. "You did say something about having an important matter 'on your plate' I guess Jeff and I are ready to find out 'what's on the menu' so to speak."

"Yes," replied Lieutenant Wilson. "You and Jeff have been involved in providing some assistance to the police on the matter of a murder at the Opera House. As you know we have been sharing certain levels of information between us. Perhaps it has been mostly one way sharing. We need to make this more of a two way sharing process."

"We are listening to your request," replied Aaron. She glanced at Jeff who was raising an eyebrow in agreement. "How can we help?"

Lieutenant Wilson nodded to Captain Smithfield at the opposite end of the table. The lead baton was being passed up the chain of command.

"As you know Ms. Worthington and Mr. Spencer," began Smithfield, "we have been pursuing several leads in the case. One of the leads has been the computer floppy disk which contains some data. That is one line or strand of the matter which brings us here together today. Another strand is that our efforts to identify any suspects in the case from forensic evidence, such as fingerprints at the crime scene or at the victim's, home have not been successful. Our interviews have not been successful. Finally, a new strand of the issue has arisen. That strand is the potential for an international terrorist action. It is this final strand which is causing the governments of Australia and the United States to come to us today. Ambassador, I believe that is your cue."

Aaron and Jeff exchanged controlled stunned looks with each other. Aaron noted that their exchanges were noted by Colonel Morgan of United States military intelligence.

"Let me add more background information to help us all understand the issue we are confronted with," said Ambassador Henry Adams. "Then Cynthia Edwards and Scott Ragsdale can take us further into some of the details we know about at this time. Joint Australian and United States military security has determined that there have been breaches of secured data bases."

"You mean the militaries have been hacked?" commented Jeff with a smirk to Aaron.

"Well, yes. To be frank we have been hacked. That is a rare event. Usually when it happens it is some teenage prankster who does something harmless like change the listed name of a piece of equipment or some such nonsense. This case is an exception. The precise nature of the breach is to alter scheduled portions of joint military exercises. In addition they have entered the files which control movement of biochemical warfare materials."

"What do you see as the implications of that kind of breach?" asked Aaron.

"We are not absolutely certain but it could mean that someone has attempted to divert or plans to try to divert the movement of chemical materials which might be used in military exercises," replied Morgan.

"What kind of chemicals are we discussing?" asked Aaron sitting forward.

"These are usually antidotal materials to combat suspected biochemical attack."

"What can these chemicals do?" asked Jeff.

"The normal function is to halt the effect of other deadly chemicals as they invade the human body. Thus, they serve as an antidote to an attack."

"Why would anyone want to get their hands on that kind of chemical?" Jeff continued to probe. "Wouldn't some kind of terrorist group want to do harm rather than stop harm?"

"Yes, but we fear the chemicals in the hands of the wrong party might be used for other purposes."

"And what might the other purposes be?" Jeff continued to probe.

"Cynthia. Explain please," asked Morgan as he turned to Cynthia Edwards.

Cynthia Edwards had been sitting listening to the exchange. Cynthia Edwards was the agricultural expert on loan to Interpol by the United States military. Her background was as a plant and agronomy researcher.

"If I can simplify the biochemistry which occurs when the chemical is activated on the body it slows down the movement of osmosis through skin pores. In effect it halts the flow of harmful chemicals which might reach the body. OK so far. No problem. But, when the same chemical is applied to many plants the effect is more dramatic and it actually completely clogs the flow of liquids through the stem of plants."

"In other words, it will cause the plants to choke and die," chimed Jeff.

"Exactly," exclaimed Cynthia with some surprise. She was surprised that her point was being understood so quickly.

"And if I understand this correctly the effect on the plant is to slowly kill the plant by producing waste by-products which appear to be rusty in nature," Jeff continued.

"Yes. How did you understand so completely so quickly?" asked Cynthia.

"Simple high school biology," replied Jeff. "No not really. Actually, I have just been developing a story on precisely that process. That is why I was so familiar with the process. I do not know the exact chemicals but I know that what you were describing, Cynthia, was just like what occurred here in Australia about six months ago up in the Darling Downs region of Queensland. It was considered a kind of stem rust. My latest research has indicated that the analysis and solution for the Queensland wheat farmers was done at Maquarie University here in the Sydney area."

"Jeff," interjected Aaron, "isn't that the same place that made the shipment of bottles which were being carried by the man who was killed in the Opera House."

"Yes," replied Jeff.

Aaron turned to Lieutenant Wilson. "Lieutenant, it seems to me that there is a connection between your murder case, the military's concern, and the story Jeff has been following. I was out to Maquarie University and talked with the scientists involved."

"Would that be Dr. Nigel Harrington?" interjected Cynthia Edwards.

"Yes, Dr. Harrington and his primary student assistant Ngarrie Bhojammie."

"I know them well," replied Cynthia Edwards. "Colonel Morgan, I know these two men would be willing to be most cooperative with us. I can vouch for their security clearance."

"Can we get them here Captain Smithfield?" Morgan asked.

Before Smithfield could reply Lieutenant Wilson interjected, "we can have them here in an hour."

"Let's plan to meet again in two hours," interjected Captain Smithfield. That will give us some time to locate them and bring any files or equipment they deem appropriate."

"Before we proceed further," spoke Jeff, "I am trying to make the connection to the computer disk which was our conceptual jumping off place."

There were several uncertain glances exchanged as people looked at other people around the room. Jeff had brought a pause so sudden that Captain Smithfield was already half way out of his chair. He paused, looked around at Ambassador Adams, and sat back down.

"Let me address the computer hacking matter," spoke Scott Ragsdale for the first time.

"We have determined that the entry into our secured systems was initiated from somewhere in the Sydney area. Further, we have determined that the changes made in the data bases were to effect the redirect movement of certain classified chemical materials." Ragsdale paused looking toward Colonel Morgan and U.S. ambassador Adams. Morgan looked at Captain Smithfield who in turn looked at Lieutenant Wilson. Aaron concluded that clearly the buck was being passed up and then back down the chain of command.

"Aaron and her associate Jeff are fully vetted in this matter. I believe we can all trust their integrity. Go ahead," Wilson said nodding to Ragsdale.

"The chemicals were of the type which, as Cynthia Edwards explained, can be used to slow down the effect of enzymes. In the redirection of one shipment we strongly suspect that someone may have made a modification of the chemical and then returned it to its intended destination."

"What destination was that," asked Aaron.

"The destination was into our joint operations in Indonesia. The redirection of a second shipment of the chemical never arrived at its intended destination. It is our suspicion that it was redirected to some other destination or destinations."

"Such as?" asked Aaron.

"We have no idea. Whatever they were doing when they hacked into our data there is no trace of where the second redirected shipment went. We have verified that it did not arrive at its intended destination."

"You said that you had traced the hacking into your data to somewhere in the Sydney area," interjected Jeff. "Can you be any more specific?"

"It is somewhere north of the harbor. We can determine that by the telephone calling area they have been using. It must be someone who is in the business of moving goods in the international trade markets."

Aaron and Jeff exchanges knowing glances. "OK, two hours back here Lieutenant," said Aaron as she and Jeff rose and exited quickly, followed by the others. Once outside of the building, Aaron stopped Jeff. "Jeff. Use my cell phone and get in touch with your friend WEB. Get him to the Bengottis place immediately. Tell him to take a taxi. We have less than two hours for him to get into their computers and find out what is going on. Somehow they must be involved in this clandestine operation." She did not say anything to Jeff about the person in civilian clothes who came out a side door of the police station and waited silently in the shadows.

Jeff took the cell phone and dialed WEB's number. He was surprised when he received an answer. "WEB. This is Jeff. Yes, I do need to know what you have found buried in the data on the floppy disk we gave you. And you are finished? Great. Listen, Aaron and I need you to meet us pronto, and I mean PRONTO. Like in fifteen minutes. Meet us at Bengottis nursery imports in St. Leonards just east of the train station. Get a taxi. Pay him up front with a big tip and tell him it is a matter of international security. OK so he won't believe you. Tell him you need to see your bookie before the next race. He will believe that and feel sorry for you. Yes. BE THERE. In TWELVE minutes." Jeff closed the cell phone and looked at Aaron. "Aaron let's go. We will need a good story for our taxi driver to get him moving as well."

"No we won't Jeff. The train. It runs ever three minutes. It will have us there in twelve minutes. Come on." And she pulled Jeff, running into Wynyard station.

# ST. LEONARDS

Aaron and Jeff were arriving in front of Bengottis Imports just as a racing taxi screeched to a halt. Out jumped William Edward Barclay. The way they almost collided had all of the characteristic of an old Keystone Kops cartoon.

William Edward Barclay was not your typical business person. He was a computer nerd. He dressed as he liked. He worked at his own pace. But, he was legendary in Australia and beyond among people who knew the world of cyberspace. He was the one they called to solve the most vexing problems. WEB, as he preferred to be called by the people he considered his friends, and Jeff went back a long ways.

"Hey, what's the 'haps'?" asked Barclay.

"The 'haps'?" said Aaron with a puzzled look.

"What's happening," explained Barclay.

"Great timing," said Jeff. "Listen WEB, you Aaron and I are going into this building. This import business belongs to three Bengotti brothers. They are having some computer problems. They have had some hackers get into their data. Their man, Harrold Lassiter, has not been able to solve it yet."

"So. What's the hurry?" asked Barclay. "I know Lassiter. he's OK. I am sure he can get it worked out soon. You called me up here for this little thing. Man, I was just writing a program to exchange data with the some martians I communicate with."

"WEB. Get serious! This IS serious."

"WEB," interjected Aaron, it is more than just Bengottis 'little problem.' We think Bengottis little problem is part of a very serious international problem which has serious implications at least for Australia and the United States. Maybe even more."

"OK. My martian friends can just wait. Open my eyes."

"There may be a connection between the hackers into Bengottis data and some hackers who have breached military security," explained Aaron. "The breach of military security

168

involves some ugly people who are getting their hands on DNA gene altering chemicals which could threaten all of us."

"I been warning those guys in the military about their loosey-goosey security," exclaimed Barclay.

"Well that is the past. We need to deal with the here and now. Now, someone is about to do something very evil. We need your help. Your government needs your help. The world needs your help. Will you help us now?" pleaded Aaron.

"Well, sure," replied Barclay with a serious look on his face for the first time since he had arrived.

They entered the building. Within seconds all three Bengotti brothers and Harrold Lassiter were greeting them in the outer office. The atmosphere was tense but friendly. The fact that Lassiter could vouch for Barclay and that Aaron clearly had the power of her connection with the police contributed to the atmosphere. Introductions were made. Harrold Lassiter and William Edward Barclay established an immediate rapport and led the others into the inner office to begin looking at data bases.

"What cha got here Las?" asked Barclay.

"Someone has hacked in and changed data," replied Lassiter as he brought up the system. "As you can see, I have identified the instances when I am sure they have broken our security. I am working on what they may have done."

Soon Lassiter and Barclay were deep into the world frequented only by computer nerds. The Bengotti brothers watched in amazement with their mouths open. They knew enough to appreciate the level of computer competency they were observing. Aaron and Jeff knew enough about what was happening to be very impressed. They looked intently as they followed along understanding much of what WEB was doing so far. This went on for about thirty minutes. The spell was broken by the bell announcing that someone had entered the outer office. Surprised, Al Bengotti went to see who was there. Soon he returned followed by Lieutenant Wilson and a plain clothes policeman.

"Well, I was wondering when you would arrive Lieutenant," chimed Aaron. "I was hoping we were not losing your man here as we rushed through Wynyard station. As you can see we are in the process of trying to unravel one of those mysteriously twisted strands of your case. Join us while WEB finds out what your computer expert and the military's computer security people have not been able to find out. Continue WEB."

"Sorry, Aaron" replied Lieutenant Wilson. "We had to move this investigation along. It is now more than just a simple murder case. There is national and international security at stake. It is imperative that we know what your sources are able to determine as quickly as possible."

They all continued to watch for another fifteen minutes as WEB, assisted by Lassiter, proceeded. Then WEB stopped and turned to Jeff.

"Jeff," said Barclay, "the people who hacked into this data base were the same people who manipulated data on that floppy disk you gave me to analyze. And, I can tell you what they have done. And, I can tell you who they are from their cookies."

"You mean they left their cookies on the floppy as well as in this data?" asked Jeff.

There were puzzled looks on the faces of Al and Frank Bengotti, Lieutenant Wilson and his plain clothes officer. They clearly did not understand 'cookies.' Jeff, Aaron, Renaldo Bengotti and, of course, Lassiter understood that they were referring to the captured unique computer signature that is left deep inside one computer by another computer which interacts with the receiving computer. It is a computer's fingerprint.

"If you have this all figured out then I want all of you, your computer, disks, and anything else Barclay needs to explain this whole thing in our station in fifty minutes" commanded Lieutenant Wilson. "We have transportation waiting outside. Let's go. We'll help you handle what ever is needed."

"What do you want me to do, Lieutenant?" asked Barclay.

"I want you to put your expertise with the expertise of the two botanic/agronomy scientists from Maquarie University and the expertise of the military security and explain what has happened. If we can solve a crime, great. If we can avert an international crises, even greater."

# SYDNEY

To say that the collection of people in Sydney Police Headquarters was unusual was an understatement. It was more like a combined international war room operation. Police vans had been pulling into the building regularly for over an hour. They were joined by military vans. They all drove into the basement bowels of the building where they unloaded cargo. The cargo was comprised of computer equipment, whole file cabinets, scientific laboratory testing equipment, boxes and briefcases of data disks, and more. Everything had been unloaded and whisked to a large meeting room on the third floor. As everything was hurriedly being set up the room took on a partial appearance of a media control room before the beginning of a major sporting event. The placement of large world maps, which had been brought in by the military, around one wall of the room, gave the added appearance of a war room.

Police, military, and government technicians were scurrying about. Helping direct equipment set up was Frank Morgan, Harrold Lassiter and Scott Ragsdale. Ambassador Adams was assisting with maps and official materials. Captain Smithfield was busy directing police personnel. William Edward Barclay had his lap top plugged in and was already reading data files while everything was hurry burly around him. Barclay seemed to be totally oblivious to all that was happening around him. In one corner, Lieutenant Wilson was conferring quietly and calmly with Aaron Worthington and Jeff Spencer. They were amazed that all this had actually taken place in the short span of two hours. As the business at hand was progressing, Major Morgan strode over to join Wilson, Worthington, and Spencer. After a brief huddling by the four, as a group they began to move around the room checking with the people involved in each set of operations. They were entering a transition from setup to analysis. It was the analysis which most interested the four.

The four, Morgan, Worthington, Wilson, and Spencer, walked across to the area where scientific equipment had been set up by Professor Nigel Harrington and his doctoral graduate assistant, Ngarrie Bhojammie. Harrington and Bhojammie were looking at computer printout material and comparing the data to samples in bottles. They were joined by Cynthia Edwards.

"Any information you can report?" asked Lieutenant Wilson.

"What we have is the historical data on laboratory and field testing of the material which produced the wheat stem rust epidemic last spring in the Darling Downs," replied Harrington. Actually we ran several tests which isolated the enzyme responsible for causing the rust problem."

"How did that work?" asked Morgan.

"The enzyme worked by confusing cell receptors into accepting the enzyme when normally the cell would have blocked the enzyme from entry into the cell. As a consequence the enzyme, which was harmful to the cell, invaded and clogged the cell so that it began to die. Essentially it was dying from the waste of its own decaying material which could not escape back into the stem."

"Tell me more about how this enzyme got into the cell," directed Morgan.

"It was the result of large amounts of a substance which in small amounts will preserve the life of plants by slowing down their life process."

"And how did that substance get into the plants?" asked Morgan.

"We looked at some seed bags. The bags had been injected with the substance. Since this substance normally effects large plants by slowing down their processes it had a more dramatic impact on seeds. The seeds are much smaller; thus, a more dramatic impact."

"Tell me, Professor Harrington, how could this substance be injected into seed bags?" asked Cynthia Edward's.

"Possibly somewhere along the shipment route of the seed bags. It would not take a huge amount injected by one or more needles in each bag. The really harmful impact on a field crop is that the impacted seeds die quickly. They exude an altered form of the substance which is picked up by normal winds which carried it across fields."

"But, my research shows that the wheat crop in the Darling Downs was saved," interjected Jeff. "Do you know how the process was stopped?"

"Yes, we do," answered Ngarrie Bhojammie. "We performed a large battery of laboratory tests on a wide range of substances. We were quite fortunate to find a compound which neutralized the chemical structure of the spreading material. It was easily applied. The majority of the crop was saved. Some fields were ruined. The Queensland government paid those farmers for their losses. It really turned out to be a great success story."

"Yes, I know," replied Jeff. "I am in the process of filing just that story. But, even more importantly, I have a colleague in the United States who tells me there is a wheat epidemic just like the one in Queensland raging through the spring wheat crop in western Kansas right now."

There were surprised looks from everyone in this part of the room. Apparently no one else knew of the apparently unrelated problem in the United States. Colonel Frank Morgan, who had been taking notes, abruptly stopped writing.

"Give me more details," commanded Morgan.

"In western Kansas the fields of young wheat plants are becoming infected by a rust type substance. It is choking the plants so the water and nutrients do not flow. And it is spreading rather rapidly from west to east which is the direction of the prevailing winds. My contact in nearby Kansas City, Missouri tells me that the agricultural experts at the University of Kansas in Lawrence have determined generally how the organism destroys the plants. However, they are still running tests to determine the specific cause in hopes they can begin later tests to experiment with a treatment process. It just sounds parallel to Queensland."

"It is exactly the same," interjected Harrington. "And I know some of the people at the University of Kansas. In fact, they have been helpful to us in setting up much of our basic research in Australia."

"I know them too," added Cynthia Edwards. "In fact I know most of them in plant and agronomy at KU. But, I am intrigued by the fact that there is a replication of this plant invading event in two countries separated by so much water. Wind from Australia can not account for the epidemic in Kansas. Perhaps if it were in Chile, but not Kansas. There is something else responsible for the transmission of the enzyme blocking agent. Something or someone is helping."

Aaron Worthington had been listening quietly to all of the discussion. She had the advantage of mentally placing everything said so far together like pieces of a puzzle. She was beginning to see a picture emerging.

*George E. Tuttle*

# WESTERN KANSAS

It was a warm early spring afternoon in western Kansas. Delbert and Rachael Kettering had returned from driving around their fields of wheat. They had reason for the happy expressions on their faces.

Martin White and Cindy Nelson had driven out to the Ketterings from Kansas City, Missouri. By interstate highway it was a four and a half hour drive. They could not be a happier couple. Cindy had just the day before won a major case in circuit court. It had been a tough case. Martin had completed the fourth of his five part series on "The Wheat Rust Scare." It was carried initially in his own paper, The Kansas City Star. It had quickly been picked up and syndicated in whole or in part by dozens of newspapers across the United States and Canada.

The four - Delbert, Rachael, Martin, and Cindy - were sitting on the Kettering verandah drinking  tea and sampling Rachael's pastries. Rachael and Cindy had been taking advantage of the opportunity to catch up on their separate lives since they were university classmates. Delbert and Martin had developed a strong friendship through the tensions of the crisis in western Kansas. Their jovial conversation about world affairs had shifted to the now ended wheat crisis.

"It must be a relief to know the crisis is over," Martin commented to Delbert and Rachael.

"Oh, yes. It is some relief," replied Delbert. "It is over and it isn't. Their are still some areas west of here in Kansas and Colorado which had 60-70 percent crop loss before the solution was found. They will need some financial help."

"Won't they get some help from the state and or federal governments," asked Cindy.

"We think so and we hope so," replied Rachael.

"What about your personal losses?" asked Martin.

"Our harvest, all things being normal now until harvest, will be down by several thousand bushels. But we will survive. Most of our fields, particularly our eastern fields, will produce almost normal yields. The spread of the stem rust was halted in time to restore nearly all of the eastern field plants. A few may be slightly damaged."

"So, just how was the crisis averted?" asked Cindy. "I have been in court so much lately I haven't even read all of Martin's stories."

"Well," began Rachael, "the plant agronomists at the University of Kansas were finally in touch with the chief plant agronomist at Maquarie University in Australia. According to the e-mail reports I have, and I believe you reported this Martin in one of your stories, the Australians had quickly found a relatively simple and very effective treatment for the condition."

"And what was that?" asked Cindy.

"The stem rust could be halted almost immediately by the application of nitrogen."

"Nitrogen?" asked Cindy with surprise. "That simple?"

"Yes. That simple," replied Rachael. "As the University of Kansas agronomists reported the Australians had quickly guessed that nitrogen would do the trick. They did some quick lab tests to determine how much nitrogen so as not to burn the plants up and still overcome the stem rust. Then they proceeded to apply the nitrogen by airplane."

"Just regular old fashioned bush pilot crop dusting," added Martin.

"OK. But, how does the nitrogen work to overcome the stem rust?"

"So simple it is scary," replied Delbert. "Once the Australians found out the harmful agent works by slowing down the cellular process causing the plant to choke on its own waste they reasoned that speeding up the cellular process would reverse the effect. Nitrogen worked beautifully."

"But, what about the spreading?" asked Cindy. I thought I recalled that the rust was spreading along with prevailing winds. How was that stopped? Nitrogen alone did not do that."

"Right," replied Rachael. The choking plant was producing an acid which was in effect a poison being spread by the wind. Stop the action in the plants, you stop the production of the poison, and there is nothing for the wind to carry. Bingo! Spreading stops."

"OK. So, how did you stop the spread Delbert? Did you use crop duster spraying?"

"Yes and no," replied Delbert. "We needed to get water loaded with nitrogen in measured amounts to the plants. Some of our fields have an auxiliary irrigation system. One of these that moves through the fields. Normally it is drawing water from a lake or from wells. In this case we attached the irrigation lines to huge tanks of mix and sprayed it at an appropriate rate across the fields. It took two passes over each field to do the job. Some of our fields do not have auxiliary irrigation systems. For those fields we had to use, as you say, bush pilot drops. There is a fellow here who helps out up in Minnesota at certain times of the year dusting their potato crops to kill the tops just before harvesting. He cleaned out his tanks and made the necessary passes over our fields. Everyone around made some kind of application."

Martin, I am a bit puzzled about how the harmful agent got into circulation," said Delbert. "I understand it was some company or group in the Sydney area who was responsible. You didn't complete that story in your series. How did it happen?"

"Right," replied Martin. "I did not explain that yet. I have only part of the story. I am including what I know in my last part of the series. It seems that this group know as Wuan Imports was using competition with another nursery business in Australia as a cover for an operation to cripple United States and Australian influence in the eastern Pacific Rim region. They had stumbled across the material Bengottis, the Sydney nursery stock importers, had developed to retard the growth of plants. It was the retarded plant growth which gave the Bengottis an advantage in delivering better plants which lasted longer. The Wuan group seized upon that opportunity to inflict environmental damage on

Australian and United States operations by creating havoc with food crops. They started with the wheat crop in Australia and followed that up with the wheat crop in the United States. They really had big plans for additional operations."

"How did they infect the plants," asked Cindy.

"We think it was by injecting the substances into some of the bags of seed. The substance was lying in the ground with the seed waiting to take hold. I am still waiting on some of the details from Jeff Spencer in Sydney before I complete my last article."

"You mentioned Jeff Spencer," interjected Rachael. "I recall he is a friend of yours. And isn't he also a friend of a woman with the Sydney Herald? Doesn't she play some major role in this whole story?"

"Indeed she does," replied Martin. "She plays THE major role. Jeff has reported to me that she is well known to the Sydney police for helping solve several previous crimes in Australia. I guess most of them murder cases. He reports that she is the one who put all the pieces together on this caper and showed the police, as well as the joint military forces, how the scheme was working. Aaron Worthington is now legend among the police and military forces of both countries."

"I didn't see much about her in your stories," commented Rachael. "Doesn't she deserve more recognition?"

"She does not want official recognition. Even the Sydney Herald stories which had the scoop on this story did not carry her name in the by-line. They carried the by-line name of an unknown. An intern I believe. Jeff reports to me that Aaron does not want a high profile recognition. She is satisfied with the value of what she has done. And beside, adds Jeff, she can work better on future cases if she isn't recognized by parties she might be investigating. She can go places and do things the police can not do. If she were well know by the general public she would lose that advantage."

"Sounds like she plans more adventures," commented Cindy.

179

"I wouldn't be surprised, based on what Jeff has related to me," said Martin.

"And what about you two?" asked Rachael. "You seem to make a perfect pair. Any plans for yourselves."

"Rachael," admonished Delbert. "You are rather blunt about personal matters, aren't you."

"Yes, I am," replied Rachael as she smiled and looked at Martin and Cindy.

"Well, we are going to try to make more time when we can do things together," replied Martin.

"We are a two career couple," replied Cindy. "I know exactly what you mean Rachael. And, no, you know I do mind your being so blunt. We have known each other too long for that. Martin and I will take time to get our lives together. Where that leads we do not know. But we do have so many common interests."

"Now. Let me turn the tables," said Cindy. "What are you and Delbert going to do next?"

"Well Cindy, we are going to finish out this harvest year first." replied Rachael. "Then when the cold winter comes to western Kansas—and believe me it is cold—we are going to take a trip down under. It will be warm summer down there"

"Australia?" asked Martin.

"Right," replied Delbert. We want to meet the agronomists at Maquarie University. We want to know what they are doing down there. And we want to visit the wheat farming region of the Darling Downs in Queensland. I really think we can share our research and agricultural techniques in ways that can benefit them and us."

# SYDNEY

Jeff Spencer and Aaron Worthington were dining in their favorite place for late afternoon lunch. They were on the balcony of the '1-2-3 Café' overlooking the shoppers in the open air Pitt Street mall between the Strand Building and the shops across from the Strand. They had finished an appetizer. They were sipping a glass from their bottle of Hardy's Queen Adelaide Riesling wine. It would last them through the rest of their leisurely lunch. Their appetizer plates contained the empty shrimp shells.

The stream of people below was steady. The late April weather was normally pleasant. Fall in Sydney is pretty and pleasant. The horrible flies of summer are gone. Leaves are beginning to show some color. Rains are light. People are out shopping. The arts season—theatre, symphony, opera—is in full swing. Aaron and Jeff had been enjoying their leisurely afternoon talking and watching the people scurry around below.

"Well, you had another exciting adventure," Jeff commented to Aaron.

"Indeed. And you were along for the ride on this one. In fact you added much to the adventure."

"Not really."

"Oh yes. Your contact, WEB, was indispensable to solving this one. And the story you were pursuing added some clues which expedited the investigation enough to prevent large scale damage."

"I am still surprised at how the whole caper worked," exclaimed Jeff.

"So am I," replied Aaron. "It all began by Wuan Imports being taken over by a group which was sympathetic to some revolutionary groups in Indonesia and Malaysia. They discovered how the Bengottis were managing to grab the bulk of the nursery market with their discovery of how to extend plant life by gene altering."

"And then Wuans used that knowledge to plot their own scheme," added Jeff.

"Right. Then they found ways to inject their concoction into seed bags. First, here in Australia, then into shipments of seeds in the United States. If these had been successful they would have gone on to other ways to disrupt a great deal of the world agriculture. The goal of the group who had control of Wuans was ultimately to foment revolution in Indonesia. It appears that East Timor was at the heart of their first efforts. But that was not the ultimate goal. They didn't care at all about independence and democracy for East Timor. That was just a vehicle for greater goals."

"Can I join this private celebration?"

"Lieutenant Wilson. Good to see you. Join us," invited Aaron. "We are just debriefing ourselves about what has happened the last few days. We just recalled how the Wuan Import operation went. But you can help us recall some of the other things which happened."

"Right," added Jeff. How did the military get involved in this case?"

"Well, it seems that the Wuans were hacking into the secret military communications operations at Pine Gap."

"Not really all that secret," commented Jeff.

"True, but not generally known. At any rate the Wuans were looking for potential ways to gain widespread distribution of the diabolical gene altered substance. It seems your friend Barclay was instrumental in helping the military locate exactly what was going on by the hackers. They were in the process of setting an invoicing control so that they could include their own parcels in shipments made by the military to its normal distribution system."

"In other words, let the military distribute their horrible stuff for them." summarized Jeff.

"Exactly. Barclay was able to determine the sequence of events which had taken place and what the next logical events would be by the hackers. The military security experts thought the hackers were trying to get control of payroll. Barclay saw that as a dodge. They were really after control of supply distribution. I must admit the military security experts were somewhat stunned when he laid it all out for them to see."

"They became believers in WEB?" asked Aaron.

"Not completely at first," replied Wilson. That happened only after we swooped down on the Wuan sites and took control of their operations. When we found clear evidence of their overall plans and tactics it was all laid out. Indeed the military was stunned. Then they became believers in what Barclay had been telling them. In fact, Barclay and the agronomists were able to determine from the data that there was a large scale operation planned."

"And how did the operation go?" asked Jeff. "Aaron was with you but I was lingering behind debriefing the agronomists on the details of the science involved."

"Oh, it was a joint move. It was planned jointly by Southfield and Morgan. The military operation was carried out by the Australian Military Terrorist Team. United States personnel were on board. And, Sydney police were on board each plane and ground vehicle used to meet the technicalities under the law. Therefore the case against these people will stand up in court."

"And you kept your word Lieutenant about giving the Herald an exclusive on this one," added Aaron.

"Of course. I promised. We appreciated your help. But none of the stories carried your name Aaron. How come?"

"Two things Lieutenant. First, I don't want that much general recognition. It might compromise my usefulness in the future. Second, a young intern needed a career boost. She worked hard on this. And she is still smarting a bit about your young officer who was feeding her controlled information. She's an idealist just out of journalism school. She feels like a 'used' journalist."

"I trust you will counsel her and help her understand how the world works."

"Oh yes. I will. The recognition she is receiving will help her feel good about the whole thing. Time will let her reflect in a reasoned manner. There must be a balance between freedom of the fourth estate and national political policy. Who knows, she may even forgive your young officer enough to continue a relationship which seemed to be beginning."

"Lieutenant," chimed Jeff, "do we know all of the details about the murder itself? That was what set this whole episode off. Why was poor mister Hutch murdered in the opera house?"

It seems that the Wuan crowd needed to remove him. He was a link to the research that had been done at Maquarie University. They wanted to remove all traces. He was carrying the computer disks and the bottles from Maquarie. So they wanted him eliminated. It was one of their henchmen who did the actual murder in the opera house."

"And he had the disk in his pocket when he went to the symphony at the Opera House. They did not know that did they?" posited Aaron.

"No they did not know that. They could not have done much about it there even if they had known. It was relatively easy to kill him. It would have been harder to get into his pockets. They fully expected to find the disk at his home. That disk contained traces of what they were up to. They knew that someone like Barclay could find that out.

"Didn't that mean that the professor and his graduate assistant at Maquarie were also in danger?" asked Aaron.

"Perhaps. We do not know for certain. But, extending the logic of what the Wuan group had already done and the reason for doing it I would say that Harrington and Bhojammie were in some danger.

"Will you join us Lieutenant," invited Jeff.

"No, I can't. Another case beckons. Thanks for your help, both of you. Perhaps our paths will cross again."

"Oh I am sure they will," answered Aaron with a smile.

Aaron and Jeff toasted each other again as the Lieutenant Wilson walked through the cafe and down the steps into the milling people along the mall below.

"OK Jeff, what about your computer friend, WEB?" asked Aaron. "What is he going to do now that this episode is over?"

"I don't know for certain. When I last saw him he was telling the military systems security people 'I told you so' and giving them a short course in the problems and solution options for data and communication security. I recall him telling them something about there is no sure fire secure system but they can reduce the odds of hackers getting in by more frequent and nearly random changing of codes. I don't know where that session was going."

"Have you heard from him at all since then?"

"Only a short e-mail thanking us for asking him to have the opportunity to perform a patriotic service. He said he would be unavailable for some time. He said something about working on a refined voice recognition language system to enable the military, and others I guess, to have almost foolproof security. I suspect that if he really wants to help them it may happen."

"And you got your stories written and into syndication."

"Yes, what I wanted to do on my own. I also sent information to Martin White in Kansas City for him to use in his series. Actually he is giving me footnote credit for a lot of his information in the series. It has worked out well."

"That leaves us, doesn't it Jeff?"

"Right."

"How much longer will you be in Australia?" asked Aaron with some apprehension in her voice.

"I plan to be in Sydney for about five or six days. Then, I want to check out some leads on a wine making process up in the Hunter Valley. That may take a few days. Then I am beginning a major research effort in New Zealand."

"Oh really. What are you going to investigate there?"

"I hear there is a new sheep cloning process underway in Hamilton. They are going to pick up where the Scots left off. Something about sheep with altered genes to improve the cleanliness and stability of the fleece. And then, I understand some ranchers up in Montana in the United States are part of this as a joint research project funded by an international corporation. That is where I will head after I leave New Zealand."

"So, we have about a week."

"I am afraid that is about it. But, I expect to be finishing this project up in July sometime in the United States. Why don't you work at clearing your calendar and meeting me in the Napa Valley? You are about due for another tour of the United States."

"It might be a challenge for me to justify the time away from the Herald." replied Aaron sadly.

"Hey, it is an election year in the United States. You could justify your trip as covering the event first hand for the Herald."

Aaron smiled. "You know, that just might fly. I will work on it."

"And tonight we have the symphony at the Opera House," noted Jeff.

Their main entree of barramundi arrived. Aaron and Jeff continued people watching below, dining, and drinking as the sun began to set. Sydney is a pretty city in the fall at sunset with a bottle of Hardy's Riesling and barramundi before the symphony at the Opera House.

## THE END

# ABOUT THE AUTHOR

Born in Kansas, Dr. George Everett Tuttle grew up in central Illinois, graduated from Illinois State Normal University and completed his Ph.D. in Speech Communication at the University of Illinois. He is Professor Emeritus of Communication at Illinois State University. After 40 years of teaching in secondary schools and in higher education he has turned his textbook and scholarly journal writing to fiction and family history writing. In Murder In The Opera House, his first novel, he takes advantage of extensive travel in Australia and through the state of Kansas, the twin plot locations in the mystery.

Mystery writing has now become an addition to a host of long time activities. Along with his wife, Joann, George Tuttle enjoys travel, ballroom dancing, photography, reading, family genealogy research, fine wine, good food, and interesting conversation wherever it may be found. Having once taught American History, Government, and Persuasion, Dr. Tuttle continues his long interest in politics.

Printed in the United States
44942LVS00002B/206